Escrow and Arrows

Rachel Lynne

Seven Oaks Press

Welcome to Sanctuary Bay, South Carolina

where the weather is hot,

the tourists are plentiful,

and the locals are half a bubble off level!

Hey y'all, I'm thrilled you've decided to journey to the South Carolina Lowcountry and tag along as Holly Daye and The Colonel solve a mystery but there are a few things I should warn you about.

On this virtual trip, you'll likely encounter 'gators, snakes, (of the critter and human kind!), balmy breezes, and endless blue skies.

You're also going to meet lots of locals! They are a charming bunch, good hearted, if a bit nosy and sometimes they speak in their native dialect: down here we just call that Southern!

Terms and phrases you might hear include *fixin' to, ain't, ain't got no, y'all, all y'all,* and of course the gold standard Southern phrase **Bless Your Heart!**

Now that last one is called upon to both wish someone well or infer their cornbread ain't done in the middle and in Sanctuary Bay it could go either way.

As far as I know, Google translate is lacking where Southern is concerned but if you get confused I'm always available to translate.

Ready to wander through the waterfront park and maybe sit a spell to watch the boats go by?

Turn the page and let the adventure begin!

Happy travels,

Rachel

Contents

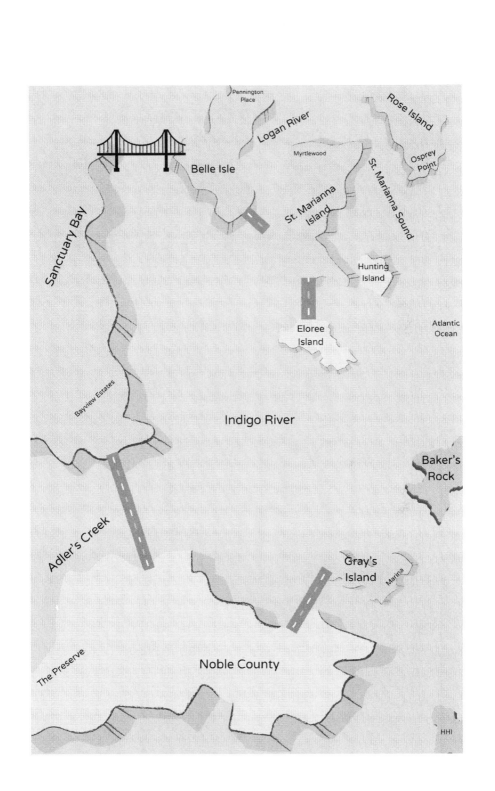

Chapter One

It was cold. Unreasonably, unseasonably cold for the Lowcountry, and any normal person would be holed up under a blanket, not running down a slippery sidewalk in high heels trying to dodge freezing raindrops.

That I was certifiable was not in question, although with Tate's dad about to enter a fist fight on the edge of the dock, I couldn't see any other options.

The Colonel, my ever-faithful English bulldog, trotted beside me, occasionally tugging at his leash in his eagerness to join the fray. With some fancy footwork, I managed to remain upright until I slid to a stop beside my boyfriend.

"Tate!" Shivering and winded, I tried to get my questions out several times before I took a deep breath and willed my heart rate back to a semblance of a steady rhythm. "What's going on? You have to stop this before someone gets hurt!"

My beleaguered boyfriend gave me a side-eye and a look that suggested my brain was frozen. "Don't you think I've tried?" Tate sighed and took a step toward his father. "Dad...this is not the time—"

"Stay out of this, Tate!" Dean Sawyer brushed his son aside and rounded on Ed Whitten, the object of his ire. "I want answers, you swindler! I put a two-hundred-thousand-dollar downpayment on a waterfront condo and seven months later I've still got nothing but a concrete pad and some pipes to show for it!"

"Mr. Sawyer..." The developer held his hands up in a stop motion. "As I've repeatedly told you, there are supply chain issues, but if you'd like to discuss this further, make an appointment because a Valentine's Day ball is hardly the place to discuss this."

A nerve in Dean's jaw pulsed as he took a step forward. "It's Doctor Sawyer and don't give me any more of that cock-and-bull story! Seven months, Whitten! Nothing is out of stock that long." He snorted. "And make an appointment? Man, I've called your office every day for over two weeks and you are *never* available."

Ed sighed and dragged a hand through his hair. "Look, I'm not going to stand out here in the freezing rain and argue with you." He turned and grabbed Ava Walker's hand. "Come on, sweetheart, I could use a drink."

Ed moved to guide his date back to the ballroom and Dr. Sawyer's eyes bulged. He grabbed Ed by the arm and growled. "Don't you walk away from me! I've invested nearly a million dollars, you cheat!"

Ed rolled his eyes and shook himself free. He met Dean's gaze, a mocking smile twisting his lips. "You're worried over a million? Some people aren't cut out for swimming with the big fish. Stick to your IRA, old man."

"Why you little—"

I gasped as Dean's hand balled into a fist. "Tate! Stop him!"

My warning came a second too late. Dr. Sawyer's fist smashed into Ed Whitten's face. The younger man staggered back, lost his footing on the slippery dock, and crashed into a storage locker.

"Get up, you slimy varmint." Dean loomed over the fallen developer. "Get up and fight like a—"

"Dad!" Tate sprung into action and pulled his father away. "Have you lost your mind? You can't go around thumping people, and what's this about you investing…"

Tate dragged his father back toward the yacht club, leaving me to help Ed to his feet and calm the semi-hysterical interior designer that was his most recent conquest.

"Get off, Ms. Daye, I'm fine!" Ed swatted my hand away and got to his feet. He brushed at the sleet and muck dotting his tuxedo pants and then made a sound of disgust. "This is a lost cause. Come on, Ava. Party is over."

"Ed, wait. What was that all about?" My questions were scattered to the wind as the smart-mouthed developer dragged Ava toward the condos at the center of the chaos.

As parties went, this one had been fraught with tension and hostility. We'd arrived at the Gray's Island Yacht Club to find environmental protestors lining the sidewalk. I felt like a scab crossing a picket line as we pushed through them to enter the ball.

The protestors weren't the only one's choosing to ignore the Valentine's Day spirit in favor of yelling at Ed Whitten. There'd been a loud and public argument in the ballroom before Dr. Sawyer's meltdown, however, his was the only one to end in violence.

Shaking my now sopping wet head, I whistled for The Colonel and gingerly made my way back to the ballroom I'd so carefully decorated. So much for Valentine's Day. Cupid's arrow had definitely missed it's mark!

Chapter Two

I found out just how bad the little cherub's aim was early the next morning while walking The Colonel.

The fight between Ed and Dean had put a damper on the party but the nail went into the coffin an hour later when the police arrived bearing news that the rain and falling temperatures were on a collision course and the roads were becoming unsafe.

Everyone had called it a night, but I'd needed to pack up my props before heading out. Even with Tate, Dean, and Mama's help it had taken more than an hour, by which time the causeway was closed due to black ice.

With no hotels on Gray's Island, we were facing an uncomfortable night sleeping in the ballroom until yacht club chairman John McGrath arrived to offer us use of the apartment above the marina office.

I'd been cozy and peacefully asleep until The Colonel announced he needed a potty break at 4:00 a.m. According to the weather app on my phone, it was twenty-six degrees, and I was trooping around on the docks in high heels and a ball gown, again.

"Colonel, hurry up and do your business!"

The wooden dock was slick and icicles hung from the trees. It was doubtful temps would warm enough to thaw the roads much before ten, so if my darn dog would shake a leg, I could catch a few more hours of shut-eye. With the number of tasks facing me in the week ahead, I needed all I could get.

"Everything is frozen, dude, you're not going to smell anything new so pick a spot!" Logic was lost on my bulldog and after another long pause while he sniffed and snorted without taking action, I gave in to the inevitable and started walking.

The sound of metal striking metal made me jump. It'd sounded like the gate I'd just walked through had been opened and closed. I looked around but didn't see anyone trooping down the dock in freezing temperatures. Still, nice to know I wasn't the only one with a screw loose.

Another glance and a flash of red near the waterfront condos suggested whoever I'd heard was sensibly retreating to a warmer environment. Wishing I could do the same, I turned my attention back to The Colonel. "You know there's no grass this way, right? Like, that was a perfectly good spot…"

I was nuts to continue a one-sided conversation, so I hunched my shoulders against the cold and let The Colonel have his head. He dragged me a few feet down the dock before deciding a stack of crab traps was fascinating.

Several minutes of aimless sniffing while I stamped my feet and wished for a pair of fuzzy socks pushed the limit of my patience. "That's it. Go now, or forever hold your pee!"

Something in my tone must have registered because my recalcitrant pup conceded and did what we'd ventured into the frozen tundra for.

"Finally!" I tugged on his leash as I turned to make my way back to the apartment. "Boy, you need me to dole out the kibble. I'd think you'd prefer I not turn into a popsicle...oh crud!"

A gust of wind tousled the hem of my dress and the delicate fabric caught on the rough wood of a piling. Reeling The Colonel back to my side, I gently tugged until the fabric was free. "Okay boy, let's go!" I started to follow him when something black waving in the wind caught my eye.

"Colonel!" I pulled him to a stop and stooped to get a better look. Just like my dress, someone else's clothing must have gotten snagged on the dock railing. Cold and in no mood to linger, I plucked the material free and shoved it into my coat pocket until I could find a trash can.

Watching for patches of ice, I set a brisk pace back to the marina office, but The Colonel had other ideas. Nose to the ground, he found something intriguing and put the full force of his tubby self into pulling me down a side path. Resigned but bitterly complaining, I trudged along as he tracked the mysterious smell.

I was absently muttering curses while watching for ice when the frost-covered dock in front of me turned darker. The

Colonel tensed and started snorting the ground, turning in circles until he found the trail.

Dark spots, some the size of a half dollar, formed a trail leading toward a boat moored at the end of the path. Coming upon a larger grouping of spots, I stopped and bent for a closer look but The Colonel surged forward, ripping the leash from my hand as he bounded toward a large yacht I was pretty sure belonged to Ed Whitten.

"Colonel! Come here!" Chest tight with fear, I scrambled after him, praying he didn't fall into the frigid water.

I breathed easier when my buddy stopped, but my anxiety ratcheted up again when he started bellowing. "Dude! People are trying to sleep!"

I doubted anyone was living on the boats moored at the newly built marina, but etiquette dictated being considerate just in case, and the yacht where he was directing his ire had lights on in the cabin.

The last thing I wanted to do on a frosty morning was get a lecture from the playboy developer. "Colonel, come!" Keeping my voice to a whisper had made my command useless, not that I thought my bulldog would have paid attention even if I'd used a bullhorn.

Picking my way toward my yammering dog, I noticed the dark stains were more frequent, and when I finally had the leash in my hand, I found the source. Propped against a storage locker across from his yacht was Ed Whitten.

Still dressed in his tux, the developer appeared to be sleeping but common sense told me that was improbable. I crept closer. "Ed? Mighty cold out..."

Seeing no reaction, I stepped closer and nudged him with the tip of my shoe. I gasped as his body fell over, exposing the source of the dark trail we'd followed. Swallowing hard, I pulled The Colonel to my side and backed away.

Ed's lifeless hand was clutched around a diving gun spear protruding from his chest, right above his heart. Cupid's arrow had finally hit the mark.

Chapter Three

My first call had been to Tate. After informing him that his services as the Noble County coroner were needed at boat slip number three, he'd spent several minutes grumbling about me always being in the wrong place at the wrong time. I'd listened with half an ear while I secured the area with rope I'd scrounged from another storage locker.

Once he'd exhausted his complaints about my penchant for finding trouble and assured me he was on the way, I'd hung up and dialed the number I was dreading.

The desk sergeant must have been a new hire because he didn't offer any chitchat before patching me through to Detective Brannon.

"Daye." His sigh rattled the phone's speaker. "Why is it always you?"

His question didn't require clarification; my reputation preceded me and I'd already heard more than enough on the subject from Tate. Jaw clenched; I mumbled a halfhearted excuse.

"I was walking The Colonel. Anyone could have stumbled upon the body, I just happened to get out of bed first."

A grunt sounded through the phone. "Uh huh, but why are you at the marina this early?"

I explained how the causeway had been closed before we could leave Gray's Island and then stewed while the detective took me to task for not obeying a police warning. Stamping my nearly frozen feet in hopes of jump-starting circulation, I almost missed the tail end of his rant.

"...headstrong...never listen..." He sighed again. "And that is why you are now stuck on the island with a dead body and no backup."

I blew on my fingers and ran back through what little I'd heard of his lecture. "Wait...no backup?"

Brannon chuckled. "Didn't listen to a word I said. Not surprising... bet you were a joy to work with," he muttered. "I said the causeway is still closed and state police reckon it'll be a few more hours before the sun is strong enough to make it passable. You're on your own, Daye."

A chirp signaled he'd disconnected the call. I glared daggers at the phone, wishing they could travel through cell towers and then stomped my way back toward the marina office.

Great. Sucked into yet another crime scene. Was there a black cloud hanging over my head? The question was rhetorical but I glanced upward anyway. At predawn, there wasn't much to see. Cloud cover suggested we'd see more rain very soon, which meant the body would have to be moved.

Tate came downstairs as I was drying The Colonel's paws and trying to thaw out.

"You left the body?"

Not liking his tone, I nodded but continued to tend to my dog. "I roped off the area, though. It's freezing and not even 6:00 a.m. Doubtful anyone else is dumb enough to be wandering the docks." I refrained from mentioning having heard someone near the docks because I shouldn't have left the body and I didn't feel like hearing another lecture.

"Just you, apparently." I glared at him as I tossed the paper towel in the trash. "I may be dumb, but would you rather I let The Colonel do his business on the floor?"

Tate held up his hand. "It's too early for this, I haven't even had coffee!" He glanced around the small office and then sighed. "No coffee pot, figures! Come on, let's get this over with."

My eyes widened. "But Brannon won't be here for a couple of hours! He said the causeway is still unsafe, so I thought we could wait..."

Tate cocked an eyebrow as I continued to stammer out my plan. He smirked and my voice trailed off into a huff. "What? Can't blame a girl for trying."

I tried to shoo The Colonel upstairs but he'd sensed I was about to leave and rushed to the door. "All right buddy, figured there was no sense in both of us freezing, but on your own head..."

Tate held the door. "After you." He glanced at The Colonel and sighed. "You know he's just going to be in the way."

Secretly agreeing, I shortened the leash and shrugged. "I'll tie him to a railing. If I leave him in here he's likely to do damage." I led the way down the docks. "Besides, you never know. Maybe he'll find the murderer and we can go back to bed!"

My stomach rolled as Tate rummaged in a storage container. I knew he was right about the body being moved, but my fingers were crossed that he wouldn't find a suitable substitute for a body bag.

"Ah hah!" He pulled a square of clear plastic from the bin. "This will work. Grab an end."

A sour taste filled my mouth as I approached Ed's body. One look at the pained expression frozen on his face made me detour. "Fine, but I'm taking the feet!"

Muttering something about amateurs that I let pass, I took my position and waited for my *boss's* instructions. "What do you think happened?"

Tate finished whatever he'd been doing to the body and snorted. "He was shot in the chest with a diver's spear gun."

I huffed. "I know that! But who could have done it? And why? We haven' t found anything to suggest—"

"And we aren't going to look." He gave me a hard stare. "You are not getting involved."

Tate waited until I nodded agreement. He'd get no argument from me. Heck, I hadn't wanted to meddle in any of the crimes I'd recently solved, things just seemed to drag me in.

"Ready?" He bent at Ed's head and nodded for me to grab his feet. "On three we'll lift him onto this plastic."

Swallowing hard, I forced myself to grab Ed's ankles. My skin crawled as I touched his cold flesh but I managed to keep it together long enough to get the job done.

Air escaped his lungs as his body connected with the hard deck surface, making a wheezing sound accompanied by a trickle of blood seeping from his mouth.

"Oh, gross." Ignoring Tate's chuckle, I studiously avoided looking at Ed's face by keeping my gaze focused on his tuxedo jacket. When Tate scooted the body a few inches something white fluttered at the edge of the lapel.

"Tate?" Grabbing the hem of my dress, I used it to cover my hand as I nudged the jacket open. "There's something in his pocket."

An exasperated sigh followed my statement. "And it can wait until I get him on the slab."

When I didn't move or respond, Tate snorted and crouched down to examine my findings. "Stubborn. Anyone ever told you—well, what have we here?"

He pulled a stack of papers from the inner jacket pocket and straightened. Based on the dark blue cover page and an official US seal, I knew what the papers contained.

"Those are passports." I stated the obvious. "Wonder why Ed was carrying them?"

"Mmm, it's his photo but look at this."

I frowned and peered over his shoulder. "What do you—oh! Who is that?" The document looked official, down to the photo. However, the name Gregory Parrish was typed in the spot where Ed's name should have been. I pointed at the other booklet in Tate's hand.

"Who does that belong to?"

My brows rose as I caught sight of the photo. Ava Walker, the pretty interior designer Ed had escorted to the Valentine's Day ball. Her passport also had a fake name.

"Gregory and Brooke Parrish." I looked at Tate. "What was Ed up to?"

I could see the spark of curiosity in his gaze but after a few seconds of looking from me to the passports, Tate shook his head. "Don't know." He got to his feet. "What I do know is it's none of our business. I'm going to wrap him up tight and call it done."

Frustrated, but also cold, I didn't protest his refusal to speculate on what we'd found. I absently watched him gather the edges of the plastic while dreaming of a warm fire and breakfast until The Colonel barked, ruining my fantasy.

He'd been good as gold while secured to the handrail, but his patience for sitting in the cold with an empty belly was at an end. The feeling was mutual. I loosened my hold on his leash and he waddled around, sniffing everything in sight. I snorted. He was probably looking for food!

"You about done, Tate? Think The Colonel is getting antsy."

My answer came in the form of a blur jogging by me. "Last one back has to rustle up some grub!"

"Hey! No fair, you got a head start and I'm in heels!"

"Likely excuse," Tate replied. "I'll spot you three feet but only if you shake a leg!"

Rolling my eyes, I turned to coax The Colonel into a trot when I noticed his jowls moving. Oh no, what had he found?

"Let's get this show on the road!"

19

"Hold on." I reeled The Colonel in and crouched down to see what he'd decided was edible. "Open up, goofy. I'm sure whatever you have isn't a substitute for breakfast."

I was wrestling with my pudgy boy when Tate returned.

"What are you doing?"

I huffed and bit back a smart remark. Wasn't it obvious? "He's got something in his mouth and I'm trying to..." With a grunt, I dragged the pudge ball closer and managed to pry his mouth open. Sticking my fingers into The Colonel's mouth, I felt around and pulled out a small piece of metal.

"What in the world? Boy, this is not food!"

"That dog! With the number of times he's scrounged something off the ground it's a wonder you aren't bankrupt from vet bills!" Tate leaned over my shoulder. "What is that?"

"No idea. Here." I handed the small silver object to him and got to my feet. "It's metal, and I think there's something written on it—Tate? Something wrong?"

He was staring at whatever I'd fished out of The Colonel's mouth.

"Tate?" He didn't reply. In fact, he showed no sign my words had registered. An uneasy feeling crept up my spine.

Tate glanced at me as I approached, then went back to staring at his hand.

"Hey, what's wrong? Thought you wanted coffee…"

His face was pale and by the way he stood staring at what I'd dug out of The Colonel's mouth, I didn't think the weather was to blame. I put my hand on his shoulder. "What's bothering you?"

By way of an answer, he asked, "Where did he find this?"

The question made me frown. What did it matter? "Uh…" I glanced around, trying to remember where The Colonel had been. "I think it was somewhere near the storage locker Ed was leaning against." My voice trailed off as realization hit.

The joke I'd made earlier about The Colonel solving the crime popped into my head. "Do you think he found a clue to the murder?"

Tate gulped and met my gaze. "Hope not. This cufflink belongs to my dad."

Chapter Four

A white knuckled grip on the counter did little to appease my irritation with Mama. However, it did help me modulate my tone before I responded.

"Mama, just let things play out. It's still early and there is no reason to assume the police won't find Ed's killer."

"But Holly!" Mama whined. "They've brought Dean in for questioning!"

I sighed. "Yes ma'am, I know. But I'm sure it is just a formality."

Mama pursed her lips. "*Just* a formality? Poor Dean's reputation will be ruined and you know how well respected he is. Why, he was doctor to half the county, and I think it is ridiculous and insulting that the police have even suggested he would do such a hideous thing!"

She cocked her head to one side and tapped her bottom lip with one perfectly manicured nail. "In fact, I think I'll call Junior and suggest he start a lawsuit for defamation..." She nodded. "Yes, that is just what I'll do, and while my grandson is handling the legal side of things, *you* can find the real killer."

The look my mother directed at me made me feel like ten tons of manure were sitting on my shoulders. Why she and so many other people in Sanctuary Bay felt entitled to enlist me in their schemes was beyond me.

A little voice in my head snidely suggested it was because I hadn't mastered delivery of the word *no*. That internal reality check made me straighten my spine and square my shoulders. I *would* resist this time!

Drawing a deep breath, I fought to keep my tone neutral. "Mama, let the police do their job. As I said, I am sure that questioning Dr. Sawyer is just a formality." I smiled to take any sting out of my words. "Why, they will probably get around to talking to everyone that attended the party. Even you."

Considering the matter at an end, I was fastening The Colonel into his harness when Mama delivered her heaviest salvo.

"Yes, they are questioning everyone in attendance at the Valentine's Day ball." Her eyes were hard as she looked at me. "But Dean is the only one called down to the station and *that* is because of Tate. Had he been a good and loyal son, this wouldn't be happening."

My mouth dropped open. "Mama! Oh my goodness, what a harsh thing to say!"

She sniffed and wiped some crumbs off the table. "The truth often is."

"That's...I mean..." I floundered for a few seconds before my brain recovered from the shock of her statement. "*Mama*, Tate had no choice but to turn that cufflink over. It was *evidence*!"

She waved a dismissive hand. "We know Dean didn't kill Ed Whitten so giving that cufflink to the police is only going to distract them from finding the real murderer." She huffed. "But, what's done is done, which is why you will have to investigate. You and Tate have seen to it that Detective Brannon is on a wild goose chase."

I blinked, shook my head, and then blinked again, but no matter what I did I could not follow my mother's convoluted logic. Common sense suggested I beat a hasty retreat and I did make it as far as the back door before my mouth ran away with me.

"Mama, I know you're upset about Dean, but I honestly don't think the police will take things any further than a few questions. There is a reasonable explanation for his cufflink being on the dock and after they realize that, they'll move on to the more pertinent evidence."

Mama's eye brows rose. "What's this? You found more evidence?"

Cursing myself for opening a can of worms, I pretended not to hear her and led The Colonel to the Scout. But Mama was on the scent and wouldn't be deterred.

I was loading the pudgy boy into the passenger seat when Mama caught up with me.

"Holly Marie, what else did you and Tate find? Will it exonerate Dean?"

Oh why had I opened my mouth? *You could have been halfway into town, Holly! Learn to keep your mouth shut!*

My inner voice was a pain in the rear, but also right. This was a mess of my own making. Hoping Mama would let it go, I moved to the driver's side door and climbed in. The door was almost closed when she pounced.

Wrapping her hand around the door frame, she tugged it from my hand. "Young lady, what did you find that will get Dean off the hook? Tell me this instant!"

"Mama..." I sighed. I was old enough to know when to raise the white flag where Mama was concerned, and I also knew I'd never get out of the driveway unless I relented. "I'll tell you, but you have to promise not to breathe a word to anyone, not even Dean!"

She pursed her lips and scowled. "I am not a gossip, Holly Marie."

"Uh...yes ma'am." Wow! There was self-delusion, and then there were the rose-colored glasses Mama wore when she looked in the mirror. Deciding not to touch the subject with a ten-foot pole, I spilled the beans. "Again, please don't say anything because it might harm the police investigation."

Mama waved her hand in a get-on-with-it motion. "Of course I'm not going to! Now what did you find?"

"Ed Whitten had two passports in his jacket pocket."

She frowned and crossed her arms over her chest. Taking advantage, I pulled the door shut and started the engine. I'd just shifted into reverse when Mama banged on the window.

Dutiful daughter that I'd been raised to be, of course I rolled it down.

"What is significant about having passports?"

"The passports had Ed's and Ava Walker's photos but the names were listed as another couple."

"And? How does that help Dean?"

A glance at the dashboard clock showed I was burning daylight and I had a long list of things I intended to accomplish. I didn't want to speculate on the murder, but if I wanted to leave...

"Mama, Ed had fake passports and he'd been staying on his yacht. If I were Detective Brannon, I'd search that boat and see if it had been outfitted for a trip. I'd also look for a link to anything criminal in Ed's life because innocent people do not buy forged documents."

Mama's mouth dropped open. No fool, I took advantage of her stupefaction and skedaddled.

Buck Randall's car dealership was scarce of people. Since I'd come to discreetly question the sales staff about some purchases made by missing county employee Preston Spruill, I couldn't decide if that was a blessing or a curse.

The Colonel was looking to do some business, so I led him toward the devil's strip and spent the time making a game plan. The events surrounding the shooting that ended my career as a Noble County sheriff's deputy had been upper most in my mind since I'd found a storage unit belonging to Preston Spruill last November.

After discussing my findings with the father of the young man I'd been accused of killing and a friend who worked as an investigative journalist for the local paper, we'd decided to make finding Preston our top priority.

While Roland and Jessica searched for clues to what had happened to the public works department manager, I was tasked with researching where Preston had purchased the dragon's horde of man toys and how he'd paid for several hundred thousand dollars' worth of merchandise on a county employee's salary.

The holiday season and several decorating jobs had kept me from focusing on the mystery but now that I'd wrapped up the

Valentine's Day ball, I was determined to put all of my energy into uncovering Spruill's secrets.

I let The Colonel lead me farther down the strip of grass bordering the dealership as I put the facts, as I knew them, in order.

Preston Spruill, assistant supervisor for the public works department had been reported missing after failing to pick his son up for a custody visit. That had been a year ago at Christmas.

Despite the police having found dinner on the table and a television blaring, the sheriff had declined to open an investigation, claiming Preston must have just decided to 'run off.'

That idea was preposterous and Jessica had tried to spur an inquiry by reporting on the man's disappearance but to date, no official case had been opened.

As much as I found the missing man's case interesting, it wasn't until Roland's trail cameras captured an image of a truck pulling into his hunting camp minutes before I arrived and the shooting occurred that Preston popped onto my radar.

A DMV search yielded a list of possible truck owners and through process of elimination, we arrived at Preston Spruill's door. I'd been cautiously optimistic we had a solid lead when his truck was a match, but when a search of the vehicle led us to a storage facility filled with expensive toys, my brain kicked into gear.

Just like Ed Whitten's forged passports led me to suspect he had been involved in illegal activities, so too did Spruill's man cave. We'd found a high-end boat, a gun safe, ATVs, and a motorcycle in his storage unit. Estimating the total value of the items in that unit were far out of the reach of a civil servant meant the man had hit the lotto or he was doing something illegal. My money was on the latter.

The Colonel exhausted the scents available outside of the dealership and I had my thoughts in order; it was show time.

I entered the showroom and feigned interest in a sleek red corvette. Within minutes I'd caught a salesman on my line.

"Hello! You'd look great behind the wheel of this baby! Care to take a test drive?"

The tall, wiry man in his midthirties turned on the charm and I could almost see him counting his commission. I smiled to ease the sting of disappointment. "Hi, she's a beauty, that's for sure, but I'm more interested in your motorcycles."

"Ah, good choice! Come this way." The light in his eyes dimmed a little, but his smile was wide as he ushered me toward the display models.

"Do you have much riding experience? At 500cc, this is a perfect bike for a beginner and I can get you out the door—"

"What about that one?" I pointed to a purple bike standing a few feet away. It was exactly like the one I'd found in Spruill's storage unit.

A flash of irritation crossed his face when I interrupted but when he turned and saw what I was interested in, his grin nearly split his face.

"You have excellent taste! This is our top-of-the-line model. Only one other like it in the county." He laid his hand on the gas tank. "It has a 988cc, four stroke engine, carbon—"

"How much?"

I'd cut into his sales spiel again, but other than a flash of annoyance in his eyes, he pivoted with aplomb.

"Ah...out the door you're looking at $59,900." He looked over his shoulder and then leaned closer and lowered his voice. "If you can pay cash, I can let this baby go for $56k."

I widened my eyes and feigned interest. "Really? Wow, that's a great deal!" Warming to my part, I bit my lip and donned what I hope was a clueless expression. "Um, I might be interested. Will you have to get a manager's approval or can we shake on that?"

The helpful salesman brushed aside my concerns. "Nah, it's a square deal. The guy that bought this bike's twin paid cash and that's the price we gave him. We're good." He gestured toward the cubicles where sales were finalized. "Let's head into my office and we can hammer out the details."

I cocked my head to the side, pretending to consider the purchase, and then schooled my features into a sad smile. "That's a lot of money, even with the discount. I read online that this model has had some problems…"

He frowned. "I'm not aware of any and really, that's as low as I can go."

"Yeah no, I'm not trying to dicker on the price, only I'd really like to hear from someone that owns one." I furrowed my brow and let him stew a moment and then widened my eyes. "Hey! Didn't you say the guy that bought one like this lives in Sanctuary Bay? Maybe I could give him a call. See how he feels about the bike after owning it awhile."

He scratched his head. "Not sure what you've been reading, but this is a solid machine. No recalls, no reported issues."

I nodded. "Well, I'd still like to talk to the other owner. Do you have his number?"

I kept my gaze steady and after a few minutes he gave in.

"Sure, I'll have to call him first. See if he's okay with me giving you his number."

"That's fine." I smiled and followed as he lead the way to his office.

We were almost there when Buck Randall and another man stepped into the hallway.

Shoot. No way Buck was gonna believe I was interested in buying a motorcycle. I was scrambling for something to say when Buck called my name.

"Holly! Nice to see you." He shook hands with whomever he'd been meeting with and then his long legs ate the distance between us. Before I had formulated a plan, he was offering his hand.

"Hey Buck, how have you been?"

The big man laughed. "Oh, can't complain, can't complain." His smile was bright, but his eyes narrowed a fraction. "What brings you here? Don't tell me you've finally decided to put your daddy's old Scout out to pasture!"

I was stammering and racking my brain for a reply when the ever-helpful salesman chimed in. "She's interested in the HR2 but wants to know if the guy we sold the other one to is happy with his purchase." He motioned toward the cubicle. "We're just on our way to look up the number..."

"Really?" Buck's gaze shifted back to me and he quirked a brow. "I'd have thought a motorcycle would be too much what with your injured leg..." He glanced down at said appendage, making me squirm. "Or are you fully recovered from your shooting?"

"Uh...I'm doing much better, thanks." I raised the hand not holding the leash and smiled. "See? No cane!"

Buck returned my smile but I noticed it wasn't reflected in his eyes. His expression turned hard as he peppered his salesman with questions, with the final one involving my request to speak to the owner of the other HR2.

The salesman explained his plan for contacting the owner who I knew to be Preston Spruill. Buck said nothing, but the frown that had deepened while they talked spread a veil of tension over the assembled, and he finally stammered through another roundabout explanation and fell silent.

There was a pregnant pause and then Buck forced a smile. "Sounds like a plan, Harry. Why don't you run and get that number for Ms. Daye while we chat."

Harry looked relieved to be excused. I didn't blame him and wished I had a similar reason to bug out. He scurried off to do his boss's bidding, leaving me the sole focus of Buck's attention.

He bent and made a fuss over The Colonel until Harry was out of earshot and then straightened to look me in the eyes.

"Why are you really here, Holly?"

He was standing far too close for my comfort and with five inches on me, he loomed in a menacing way. But I was made of sterner stuff, or maybe I was just stupid. Either way, I pinned a bright smile to my face and tried to look as innocent as was possible for me.

I forced a light laugh. "I told you, Buck. I'm thinking it's time to hit the open road, wind in my hair, sun on my face, maybe a side car for The Colonel?" I shrugged. "Blame it on mid-life crisis."

He snorted and I knew he didn't buy my act for a second.

He crossed his arms over his chest and looked down his nose. "You expect me to believe you want to start riding. After what happened to your cousin, I find that very hard to believe."

Drat. That was one of the many problems with living in a town where everyone knew everyone else and your family business was spread all over the county. My second cousin on Daddy's side had been a bit of a black sheep.

Dale was an avid motorcyclist and philanthropist. He organized poker runs for charity and always led the pack on the rides, until the day a car crossed the center line. My cousin had suffered a severe head injury and lived on life support for two years before his family had accepted the inevitable. No, Buck was absolutely right. I had no interest in riding.

Knowing when to hold 'em and when to fold 'em was not just a useful poker skill. "You're right, I didn't come here to buy a bike."

His brows rose. "I see. Since you've already stated you aren't in the market for a new truck, why are you here?"

His tone was guarded and I watched him closely as I explained. "Callie Spruill has asked me to help her track down her husband."

"A missing husband?" A chuckle escaped him. "Read about you solving some murders recently. You runnin' a private eye business along with your decorating?"

My answering smile was tight. "Nothing like that. Just helpin' a friend."

"That's nice. Wish I...uh, wish that I could help but um...Spruill? Not sure I know who that is." He kept up the jovial tone, but I hadn't missed him tense when I'd mentioned Callie's last name.

As a cop, I'd been trained to watch body language, and Buck's was screaming discomfort, and along with his fumbling for words, my radar was going off.

Judging by his non-verbal clues, I guessed Buck knew more than he was saying, but I played along. "Oh, surely you remember, Buck. It was just before Christmas, the year before last. Assistant public works director missing under mysterious circumstances?"

He cleared his throat. "Oh! Uh...I might have heard about that. But um..." Buck gave a nervous laugh. "Not sure how anyone at my dealership can help with that."

"Harry already did." Buck's eyes widened and a slight tremor in his hands told me that news was not welcomed. But, I had to hand it to him, his voice reflected no agitation.

"Good, glad we could be of help. If that's all then? I have to make a call..." He started to walk away and then stopped to look back at me. "Uh, just out of curiosity, how did Harry help your investigation?"

I smiled politely, but Buck's nervousness had me on alert. "Callie and I found a storage unit owned by her husband. It was filled with expensive man toys and we wondered how he'd managed to buy them on a county employee salary. Finding out he paid cash for the HR2 is eye opening." I watched him closely. "Definitely sets on us a new path, don't you think?"

Oh that had certainly rattled Buck! He paled and swallowed convulsively a couple of times before managing to smile. He shrugged nonchalantly. "Wow, that is interesting. But, as far as we're concerned. The sale was above board." He waved. "Now, I need to make that call so if there's nothing else?"

My grin was wide and far more enthusiastic than the circumstances warranted. "Nope, not a thing. Thanks for your help, Buck. Have a great day!"

I watched Buck out of the corner of my eye as I pretended to adjust The Colonel's harness. He held the phone up to his ear and a benign smile was on his face, but he was watching me like a hawk. I felt his gaze on me as I left the dealership and wondered if my investigation into the disappearance of Preston Spruill was the topic of his conversation.

Questions were tumbling through my brain as I loaded The Colonel into the Scout, not the least of which was, why had my inquiry about Preston Spruill made Buck so nervous?

Weighing what little we knew about the disappearance of Preston Spruill and how he fit into the puzzle that was the shooting that had ended my career, I guided the truck toward my office, intent on calling Roland and Jessica.

Normally, if I had a problem to solve, I talked things over with my best friend and partner, Connie. But her father had passed last week and she'd went to Ohio to settle his estate.

I'd just parked in CoaStyle's lot when I got the first phone call destined to ruin my day.

Chapter Five

P icking my way across the soggy lawn, I found four men diligently digging a trench in the side yard of Myrtlewood, my family's plantation. I was about to approach and find out which man was the plumber when my brother Dewey came out of the house.

"Holly!" Dewey stalked toward me, a scowl on his face. "You know which trunk Mama's wedding stuff is in?"

Frowning, I tried and failed to connect my mother's keepsakes to the broken pipe currently flooding our yard. Rolling my eyes, I met Dewey half way. "How much is this going to cost?"

Dewey shrugged. "Don't know. I got the guy's number from Jed. Didn't ask no questions about price. Was just happy they could come right out!"

Of all the...leave it to my brother to hire the first person he called. Why should he be concerned with cost? It was no skin off his nose. I said the quiet part out loud and Dewey bristled.

"Oh that's nice. Ya oughta be grateful I found the dern leak 'afore it flooded the house!"

He had me there, though his comment made me frown. "Yeah, but why did you come out here? Thought this was your day off."

He huffed. "It is fat lot of difference that made to Mama! She asked me to come find some trunk or other she swears is in the attic but I'm danged if I can find it. Can you go look?"

I wrinkled my nose. "What? No, I've got to deal with this broken pipe!" I returned to watching the men work. "Is that what you were hollerin' about a minute ago? I heard something about wedding stuff."

Dewey sighed. "Yes. Mama wants her crown or somethin'."

"A crown? Why would our mother own a crown?"

Dewey scoffed. "Heck, I don't know! All she said was it's got pearls on it and she wants to lend it to Alexis." His tone morphed into a whine. "Can't you go find it? It's your future daughter-in-law!"

Enlightenment dawned. "Tiara, Dewey. Mama wore a tiara with her veil, not a crown."

He snorted. "Whatever. I ain't qualified to look fer somethin' like that. You go find it and I'll deal with the plumber."

Since Brooks Junior and Alexis weren't getting married until April, finding the tiara was not high on my priority list. "It can wait"—Dewey's eyes bulged causing me to smirk—"and yes, I'll square it with Mama."

Not knowing what I'd find in the yard, I'd left The Colonel in the truck and now I was getting worried he'd do something destructive to my upholstery. I turned on my heel. "Be right back, I'm gonna get The Colonel..."

A shout stopped me in my tracks. I turned to see the work crew gesticulating and chattering as they backed away from the trench.

"Oh, what now?" Dewey and I started toward the men but the supervisor met us half way.

"Afternoon ma'am, Bruce Lidner." He swiped his hand down the front of his jeans and then offered it to me. "'Fraid we're gonna have to call the coroner."

I stopped mid-handshake. "Wha— The coroner?" Bruce nodded. "What on earth do you need the coroner for?"

Resting his arm on his shovel handle, he pointed toward the trench. "That's the law, ma'am. We done struck bones."

My eyes widened. "Bones? You've dug up bones?" Without waiting for a reply, I hurried over and peered into the hole they'd dug. Sure enough, part of a bone was sticking out of the dirt.

Footsteps crunching on the dead grass made me turn. Dewey and Bruce had followed me. I glanced up and told Dewey to fetch a broom from the shed.

While my brother did my bidding, I dealt with Bruce. "I'll take care of this, y'all go on with fixin' that pipe."

He shook his head. "Can't do that, ma'am. Law says—"

"Yes, I'm aware of the law but we don't even know if these are human remains. For all we know, it's one of my ancestors' pets." I looked back at the trench and frowned. "Why are y'all digging here, anyway? Wouldn't the water main run in a straight line from the house to the well pump?"

His eyes widened as my question sank in. He scratched his head and nodded. "Guess we got off course a bit, sorry about that. We'll put the sod back after the coroner comes..."

Biting my tongue to hold back the string of curse words begging to be released, I pointed toward the well pump. "I'll make the call to the authorities. Y'all start fixin' that pipe."

How had they not realized...I stopped that train of thought in its tracks before I ruptured a blood vessel. What was done was done. I sighed and pulled out my phone. I'd just finished texting Tate when Dewey came back with the broom.

"What ya want this for?"

Instead of answering, I started brushing soil away from the bone protruding from the side of the trench. I'd been hoping to find a small bone consistent with an animal but when a large clump of dirt fell away exposing a rib cage along with several other bones, those hopes were dashed; my limited medical knowledge said the long bone was a femur and unless six-foot-tall animals had once roamed the plantation, it had belonged to a human.

I handed the broom to Dewey and got to my feet. "We'll have to wait for Tate."

Dewey's eyes widened and he backed away. "It's human? A human being is buried down there?"

I rolled my eyes. "Yes, it's a human leg bone, but calm down. There's no need to—"

"Calm down?" He threw up his hands. "You been stickin' yer nose into too much crime if ya think there's nothing to freak out about. A person's been murdered and buried on our land!"

My phone chimed a reply from Tate. I typed the particulars of the situation to him as I lectured my brother. "Dewey, this plantation has been here since the 1700s. I'm sure they buried their dead on the property and I'm equally sure these remains are old." I glanced at him. "Really, really old most likely and they probably died of natural causes."

Unable to argue with my logic, Dewey started for the shed, muttering about dead bodies and ghoulish sisters under his breath. A few more text messages to Tate and I had his assurances a forensic team would be dispatched.

I was debating the wisdom of leaving Dewey to wait on them when my phone rang. Seeing the caller ID I sucked in a breath. Why was the Noble County Sheriff's office calling me?

"Hello?"

"Hello, this is Officer Tammy Prater. I'm looking for Ms. Holly Daye."

Ah crud, this couldn't be good. Wincing, I replied. "This is she. How can I help you?"

The officer cleared her throat. "Ma'am, you're mother has been detained for trespassing."

Assuring the officer I was on my way, I ended the second call destined to wreck my day.

Chapter Six

G ripping the steering wheel so hard my knuckles were white, I tried to tune out Mama's excited chatter. She was rattling on about something she'd overheard at the sheriff's office, but I was too stunned to care.

My mother had been arrested! The snide voice that resided within me pointed out that Mama had merely been detained but it was all semantics. For all intents and purposes, Euphemia Sinclair Barker had been hauled into the pokey! At my age, it was doubtful I'd ever fully recover from the shock.

My mind was running in circles and driving home was accomplished purely by muscle memory. Despite my mother's blasé attitude on the subject, we were going to have words. Just as soon as I wasn't behind the wheel.

"...and while I'm on the subject." Mama turned in her seat and looked at me. "When was the last time the sheriff's department was updated?" She tsked and flopped back into her seat. "With all of the taxes we pay, you'd think someone would apply a bit of money to that building. Why, the table in that...that whatever they call it room was scarred and there were stains on the chair cushions! I dusted it off before I sat but I fear my beige slacks are the worse for wear." She huffed. "Holly Marie, are you listening to me?"

"Interrogation room, Mama." I guided the truck through a curve and flipped on my turn signal. Contrary to what my mother believed; I'd heard every word she'd uttered. I was simply incapable of forming a coherent reply, and under the circumstances, who could blame me?

Mama had moved on to dinner plans and I caught something about a garden club meeting but I let it all run in one ear and out the other as I parked the Scout and wrestled The Colonel out of the back seat. I was reaching for the remote control that closed the gates when Tate pulled in.

By the time I'd helped Mama out, Tate had joined us. One look at his face showed something was terribly wrong.

"Tate! What's happened? You're as pale as death!"

He sighed and started to reply but Mama shivered and grabbed his arm. "Come inside and tell us. It's far too cold to be nattering on out here!"

Once in the living room, Tate began to pace. He looked haggard and bedraggled, and I wondered if he'd slept in the last twenty-four hours. "Tate, come sit down." I patted the cushion beside me. "Whatever it is can't be that bad—"

"They've arrested Dad! It can't get any worse than that!"

I gasped and my stomach dropped. Mama clutched her chest and sank into her chair muttering "good gracious."

The outburst seemed to drain the last bit of energy from Tate. He wilted and dropped onto the sofa beside me, holding his head in his hands.

"Tate…" I sighed and patted his shoulder thinking how ineffectual I was where emotions were concerned. I was more suited to action, but in this instance there was nothing I could do. "I'm sure it will all smooth out. Surely they can't believe a cufflink is enough evidence to go to trial..."

Tate looked at me like I was deranged and I had to admit, my comment had been pretty lame. I'd worked for the Noble County Sheriff's Department for over twenty-five years and had nothing but good things to say about most of my colleagues. Detective Joe Brannon, however, was not one of those that I sang praises over. He'd improved somewhat over the past year, even going so far as to thank me for solving the murder of a priest when his hands were tied by politics.

But overall, he was still the position- and status-hungry man I'd met just before the shooting that ended my career. I had no faith in him treating this case differently than the others; he would take the easiest route and call it good.

I started to offer comfort, however trite it might be, but Mama beat me to the punch.

"Now then, sitting around with long faces is of no help to Dean." She directed an expectant gaze toward me. "What's our plan, Holly Marie?"

"Plan?" I blinked and shook my head, though neither action brought clarity. "What are we supposed to be planning?"

Mama huffed and looked at Tate. "Do you see what I have to put up with?" She waved a dismissive hand. "Pay attention, Holly. Dean's been arrested and we must find the real killer! Now, I've already started inquiries and...young lady, why are you staring at me like I've grown two heads?"

Swallowing several times while my gaze bounced between my mother and my boyfriend, my mind ran through all that had happened from the time I found Ed's body to my springing Mama from jail.

I replayed what Mama had just said, the words "already started" flashing in my head like a neon sign. All the shock, worry, and fear brought on by the phone call from the sheriff's office solidified and my tone was anything but respectful as the words came tumbling from my mouth.

"Mama, are you telling me you've been investigating Ed Whitten's murder?"

"Well yes, of course I have!" She was primly sitting in her chair looking like butter wouldn't melt in her mouth and I found myself floundering again.

"But...I mean..." I stammered as I absorbed what she was telling me and then a light bulb went off. "That's why you were trespassing on Ed's yacht?"

Her patronizing smile suggested I was a little bit slow. "How else was I to hunt for clues?"

"Clues..." Dumbfounded, I shook my head and stared off into space. My mother was running around playing detective and getting herself arrested. Next she'd be talking like a private dick from a noir film, brandishing her heater, and calling people "dirty rats"!

I drew a deep breath, released it slowly and then repeated the process; it didn't help. "Have you lost your mind? For all you know, that boat is a crime scene, or worse, you could have run into the killer!" Finally allowed free rein, all the emotions I'd suppressed since getting the call to pick her up at the station bubbled over and coalesced into outrage.

Full of nervous energy, I leaped to my feet and started pacing. "Of all the harebrained, nonsensical..." Hands on my hips, I turned to look at her. "Whatever put such a crazy notion into your head?"

Mama's brows rose. "Why, you did, dear."

A bark of laughter made me glare at Tate. I was about to take him to task when Mama's rambling derailed me.

"And I must say that it was a good one, too! Do you know, I expected Ed's yacht to be nicer on account of how flashy he was.

But the upholstery in the salon was shabby and that pattern!" She tsked and shook her head. "Tacky! And those cushions are very poor quality. Why, they crunched when I sat on them!" She sighed. "Just goes to show money doesn't buy class. The floors were nice though. A lovely mahogany, as were the walls and trim. Now I do think the master bathroom was a bit cramped, but I daresay that can't be helped on a boat—"

"Mama!" I'd reached my tolerance for the absurd. "Enough about that boat! Do you have any idea what you've done?"

"Oh, that." She waved a hand in dismissal of my concerns. "Sheriff Felton said they won't press charges and all he did was warn me not to be a nosey parker in future."

"A nosey..." I blew out a breath and wondered if my blood pressure was near stroke levels. "Mama, you contaminated a crime scene! You're lucky they gave you a warning. You do know you can do jail time for that, right?"

She snorted. "Oh, don't be silly." She cocked her head to one side and mused. "I will admit I shouldn't have gone when I did." Eyes shining with excitement, she met my gaze. "Next time, we'll go after dark!"

"What?" I looked at Tate, hoping for support but he just shrugged. Men! "Mama, there will be no next time!" I peered at her and frowned. "At the risk of repeating myself, have you lost your mind? Are you forgetting things lately, or..."

She bristled. "I resent that, young lady. I'm not senile. What's more, I knew exactly what I was doing, *and* why!" She leaned forward, a pleading expression in her eyes. "Holly Marie, we *have* to help Dean!"

Mama fussin' at me I could just about resist but she was pleading with me and there were tears in her eyes. I sighed and considered what she was asking of me.

I'd stuck my nose into murder cases several times now and been successful. But investigating often put me in harm's way and Tate had lectured me about minding my own business many times; it had become a bone of contention in our relationship.

Now it was Tate's father in the hot seat...I looked at him and quirked a brow. Giving me a rueful smile, he correctly interpreted my silent question.

"Ms. Effie is right, Holly. I know I've given you a hard time about playing detective but...I have little faith in Brannon and there's no one else." He sighed. "I hate to ask you to put yourself into potential danger but I'm out of options." He rose and took my hand. "Will you help me find Ed's killer?"

Before I could reply, Mama chirped. "Of course we will!"

Tate flashed me an amused smile and I mouthed the word *yes*.

He gave me a peck on the cheek and sat down. "I have no idea where to start. I'm out of my element without the forensics…"

The neighboring county's coroner had taken over when Tate's dad became the prime suspect. The loss of that information could stymy our search, but it couldn't be helped.

"That's all right. It's nice when I can ask you for insider info but we'll manage. Since we were first on the scene, we probably know as much as the coroner does. I just wish I knew if the police got anything off the marina cameras, assuming they have them."

Tate shrugged. "They do but they aren't operational yet since the marina is still technically under construction. But, we know he was killed by a shot through the chest with a spear gun and I did do a preliminary examination before I was taken off the case, so we know the estimated time of death is between 1:00 a.m. and 3:00 a.m."

My eyes widened. "Oh, that is very helpful! So we know when he was likely killed and we know he had forged passports. Now we need a list of people that had access to the yacht club marina that morning and also had a reason to kill Ed." I was trying to be optimistic but in truth, I was worried. There were a lotta people at the ball that night and we had no clues other than the passports and the cufflinks.

"We can start with what we know," I sighed. "But I wish we could have searched the yacht..."

Mama huffed. "I did a thorough job, you know."

"I'm sure you did, Mama. It's just that another set of eyes is always helpful, and I'm trained to look beyond the obvious. No matter, we'll make it work. Just would have been nice if Ed had left us a clue about what he was up to."

"I did find something interesting." She dug in her pocket book and pulled out a glossy brochure. "It was on the side table in the salon and someone wrote a date and time on it. Do you think it's a clue?"

I frowned and held out my hand. "Let me see."

A standard trifold brochure advertising the Paradise Harbor marina complex in Aruba, each page was filled with pictures of exotic locations along with a list of amenities the resort offered.

I opened the pamphlet and saw the scribbles Mama had mentioned. A date ten days from now was written in the upper right-hand corner along with a time of 4:00 p.m. The marina's phone number had also been circled.

Ed's yacht was a sixty-foot Azimut and I'd estimate it was capable of doing about thirty knots. He would burn a lot of fuel running that hard, but if he cruised at ten to thirteen knots it'd take about a week, week and a half to reach the western Caribbean.

Grinning, I closed the brochure and tapped it on the edge of the coffee table. "I know where to start."

Chapter Seven

For the fourth time in less than an hour, I wondered what god I'd ticked off and what I'd have to do to appease it.

"I still don't see why we didn't split up!" Mama huffed. "I could have been looking for clues or questioning the suspects while you do whatever it is you find more important than saving Dean!"

Gritting my teeth, I downshifted and eased into the Canary Wharf parking lot before responding. I jerked the parking brake upright and twisted to face her.

"Mama, for the last time. You are not, I repeat NOT, going to go poking around by yourself. In case it's escaped your notice, we are hunting for a murderer." I left her stewing in the passenger seat while I hauled The Colonel out.

"And another thing," I said as I helped her out of the truck. "Who are these suspects you want to interview? And where are you planning to look for these clues?"

Her lips pursed. "As to that, I'm not quite sure. But we have to do something!"

"Yes ma'am, I agree." I held the door to Glitter and Garland craft store and ushered her inside. "And we will do something, just as soon as I've checked on the store. I promised Connie I'd keep an eye on things while she's in Ohio." I lowered my voice. "You know Missy hasn't been working here that long and Mike only handles deliveries. It's hard enough dealing with the death of your father. Connie shouldn't have to worry about her store, too. Now go through to my office and I'll be with you in a few minutes."

Surprisingly, Mama did as I'd instructed, though I hadn't missed her sniff of disapproval. Tough. She'd insisted on helping me find Ed's killer, she'd have to learn who was in charge.

Missy finished ringing up a customer's purchases and then bent to pet The Colonel. "Mornin' Holly. What brings you in?"

"Hey Missy. Just checkin' in. Everything going okay?"

She nodded. "Yep. Had a big rush for Valentine's Day but we've been pretty quiet since then." She nodded to a stack of boxes sitting outside of the storeroom. "In between customers, I'm adding the stuff Connie bought for Easter into inventory. Come see!" She started rummaging through the boxes. "Look at these napkin rings with the decoupaged oyster shells and these...these are my favorites!"

I smiled at the sea shells glued into egg shapes and admired the polished oyster shell garlands and napkin rings painted with traditional Easter themes. "Adorable. Bet they sell like hot cakes." I glanced around and noticed a perishable box sitting on the workbench. "Are those the bridal party bouquets for Lindy Martin?"

"Yeah, don't worry. They've only been out of the cooler a few minutes. Mike is going to run them over to the church just as soon as the van warms up."

"Okay, sounds like y'all have everything under control." I nudged The Colonel into motion and headed for the back door.

"I'll be in the CoaStyle office for about an hour but after that, you can reach me on my phone."

Assured everything at Glitter and Garlands was running properly, I went next door where I found my mother rummaging through my desk drawers.

"What are you looking for?"

She jumped and scowled at me. "I need to put a bell around your neck. You scared me to death!" She perched on the edge of a chair and pointed at my desk chair. "Sit down and let's get to work."

It was rarely worth arguing with Mama, so after I filled The Colonel's water bowl and handed him a busy bone, I did as commanded.

She quirked a brow and gave me an expectant look.

"What? Did you want something?"

"Holly Marie," Mama huffed and sat back in her chair. "I'm waiting to hear your plan."

Desperately wanting to roll my eyes, I refrained out of fear of a scold and got down to business. "All right, when I've done this before, Connie usually helps by making a list." I pulled out a piece of paper and slid it across the desk, along with an ink pen.

I pointed at the paper. "Make a T shape down the page and label the first column 'Suspects' and the second one 'Motive.'"

Mama started to draw but with a line half way down the middle of the page, she stopped and looked at me. "Don't we need three columns?"

As I'd stated, list making was Connie's domain. I shrugged. "What would go in the third column?"

Mama huffed. "Clues! We need a place to list the clues we find."

She had a point. "Okay, do it that way then, and put forged passports, the cufflink, and the Aruba marina under clues."

My mother used her beautiful penmanship to follow instructions and then tapped her pen on the desk. "Is that all we have by way of clues?" She frowned and tapped her pen on the desk. "How is this pitiful list gonna save Dean?"

I rolled my eyes heavenward and prayed for guidance because only the Lord knew how I was gonna survive workin' with Mama. I started to reply when The Colonel caught my eye.

He'd carried his bone over to the couch and was now sniffing around the coat I'd tossed over the back. "Boy…" Thinking I might have left a piece of candy or a mint in one of the coat pockets, I jumped up but not fast enough. Before I could reach him, The Colonel pulled my coat down and started digging at it.

"Hey, cut that out!"

"What on earth is that dog doing? He'll tear the upholstery..."

"Colonel, stop that!" I reached the couch just as he lifted his head and flashed a big bulldog grin. My eyes narrowed. He'd had a busy bone a minute ago... "Where's the bone, buddy?"

Something had gotten into my boy because he dropped into his yoga pose and wiggled; a sure sign he anticipated a game of fetch. I patted his head. "Sorry boy, it's work time. Now where did you put that bone?"

"It's probably between the cushions."

I nodded to acknowledge Mama but I'd already checked there. I was about to give it up for a lost cause when it hit me. The Colonel wanted to play fetch, and thanks to Dewey buying him an automatic ball thrower, my bulldog now thought his toys would launch from anything he dropped them into.

With a laugh, I pulled the busy bone out of my coat pocket and tossed it across the room. The Colonel chased after it, and to forestall a repeat performance, I decided to hang my coat up. I shook the dog hair off before slipping it over the hanger and something fluttered to the floor.

"What's that, Holly Marie?"

I cocked my head to one side and frowned down at the bit of black fabric...then it hit me. "I don't know what it is, Mama, but I found it caught on a piling near where we found Ed's body."

I picked the piece of black cloth up and returned to my chair. "Any idea what it might be from?" I tossed the fabric scrap to Mama.

"Hmm, it appears to be silk and whatever garment it's from, they used a French hem."

Apart from the word silk, I was completely lost. "Uh, in laymen's terms, what does that mean?"

Mama smirked. "It means, my fashion-ignorant daughter, that this was most likely part of an expensive outfit. Likely custom tailored." She studied the swatch, turning it over in her hand and then laying it out on the desk. "You know, it's possible this was part of a bow tie."

"You think?"

Mama nodded. "I do, and not one of those that come pre-tied." She pointed to the end of the fabric where the fancy stitching remained. "My guess is that this was part of an expensive tuxedo."

Expensive. I took that to mean not a rented tux. "Running with your theory, what men were wearing those kinds of tuxedos?"

I had no doubt my fashion and appearance conscious mother would have noticed what the men at the ball were wearing and she didn't disappoint.

"Charles Tomlin has a bespoke tuxedo, he wears it to all the formal dos, and Dean's was also a tailored ensemble. It's not uncommon for professional men of that age group to own quality formal wear." She tapped her bottom lip with the end of the ink pen. "I noticed Todd Rudd was wearing a very nice tuxedo and of course Ed Whitten did." She glanced at me. "Does that help? I'm sure there were others of course, but those are who I particularly noticed."

"Eh…" I scrunched my nose and considered the information "If it is part of a bow tie, it's probably Ed's. I wonder if Tate can find out the state of Ed's clothing."

Mama's eyes widened. "Is it a clue then? Shall I add it to our list?"

Her enthusiasm made me want to laugh. I managed to contain myself and nodded. "Put black fabric under the other clues. I'll see if Tate can confirm whether or not it belonged to Ed, but if it does I am not seeing how it helps us find his killer."

"All in good time dear." Mama wrote what I'd instructed and then gave me an expectant look. "Now then, let's move on to suspects. Who do you think did it?"

Once again, I suppressed the urge to laugh. Was I supposed to pull names out of a hat? "Mama, I have no idea who might have killed Ed—"

"Well that's not going to get Dean off the hook! You must have some idea..."

"Not really." I considered what I knew of Ed Whitten. He was the owner of Royal Ventures Investment Bank. He found investment opportunities for his clients, and in recent years, he'd expanded to real estate development.

Ed had also been a notorious playboy. Married three times, and according to rumors, paying eye-popping alimony, he'd confined himself to dating after wife number three took him to the cleaners. Thrice burned but not shy, Ed seemed to have a different woman in his life every other month.

Thinking back over the past year, I seemed to recall him dating several different women, but since I didn't listen to or spread gossip, I couldn't put names to faces. Changing partners quicker than people changed the batteries in a smoke detector was bound to have caused hard feelings.

"Mama, under motive put down jilted lover."

Her brows rose but she did as requested. "You think one of his women did him in?" She answered her own question. "It's not farfetched, I'll give you that. I know of two women he tossed aside and both were bad mouthing him because of it."

Oooh, a gossip queen for a mother had its uses! "Who were they, Mama?"

"Hmm? Oh, well one was a doctor from Charleston? Or maybe it was Columbia. Either way, that was over a year ago not long after his third divorce was finalized. They were hot and heavy and the ladies were taking bets on her becoming the fourth Mrs. Whitten but nothing ever came of it."

I snorted. "Ed was contemplating another walk down the aisle? He must really like paying alimony."

Mama smiled. "Perhaps it's one of those fetish things." I laughed and was about to ask my mother what she knew of such things when she frowned and licked her lip. "Speaking of alimony...I wonder if that is why all of Ed's women are now career types?"

I frowned. "I don't follow..."

"Oh, well it's just like you said. He's paying to keep three ex-wives in the style they became accustomed to because none of them were women that worked outside of the home. Seems he's sticking to ladies who can't claim total dependence after the breakup."

I grinned. "That makes a lot of sense and probably why he loves them and leaves them."

She nodded absently and I could see her wheels turning. "What are you thinking, Mama?"

She blinked away the puzzled frown. "Talking about Ed's matrimonial plans reminded me. There was another woman he dated...it was while you were recovering from the um..." She glanced at my leg and shuddered. "I was preoccupied at the time but do recall their public fights had tongues wagging. I'll ask Lou Lou or Maybelle if they remember who the woman was, but regardless, I do know she was angry because Ed led her on and then didn't close the deal."

"Great. Once you get a name, we can compare it to the guest list for the ball." Jealousy was a powerful motive and the way Ed played the field suspects should be thick on the ground. "Now, were any of his other ex-lovers at the Valentine's Day gala?"

Mama scribbled something onto the list and then propped her chin in her hand. "Well, Stephanie Gilroy was there..."

My brows rose. "She dated Ed?"

"Oh my yes! How can you not know that?" She rolled her eyes. "It was around May or June of last year. I never did hear what happened, but Stephanie was providing lots of fodder for the gossip mill." Mama shook her head. "I always thought that was a case of the pot meeting the kettle because Stephanie is notorious for chewing men up and spitting them out!"

No truer words. The preeminent real estate broker in Noble County, Stephanie was the sister to Whopper, who happened to be my brother's best friend since kindergarten.

Because of that relationship, I'd been admonished to *play nice,* but she was the quintessential mean girl and had been the bane of many people's lives all through school—including me.

I could definitely see Stephanie shooting Ed with a spear gun. "I think I saw her schmoozing with the big wigs."

"Oh yes, she most certainly was! But that's no surprise. She's always been a social climber." Mama warmed up to her character assassination if the word character could be applied to Stephanie.

"She made a fool of herself, flirting with Todd Rudd. Everyone knows the man is madly in love with his wife...and that dress! Gracious, a woman in her fifties ought to know better than to parade around in a skin tight dress that barely covers her behind."

"Yes ma'am." No matter my dislike of the realtor, I had no desire to talk about her behind her back; I'd tell her to her face if necessary. "Her being a less than stellar person with questionable fashion sense isn't enough to suspect her of murder, though."

Mama snorted. "Maybe not but considering her past affair with Ed and then that dreadful scene..." She sighed and clicked her tongue. "But what can you expect with a mother like hers."

I winced and searched for a way to change the subject. Mama and Dean's first date had been scuttled when Ruby Gilroy, Stephanie's mother, had caused a scene at Ms. Lou Lou's garden party. It had ended with Dean covered in sweet tea and Mama humiliated. Nope, definitely not going there!

I frowned and cast my mind back to the night of the ball. With everything that had happened, I'd forgotten that Stephanie had caused a scene. "She fits the jilted lover motive, and I recall loud voices and everyone staring at Ed, but I was heading outside to walk The Colonel and didn't see who the instigator was. Was Stephanie layin' into Ed about him dumping her?"

"Hmm? Oh, no I don't believe so. I couldn't make out much of what she was shrieking but I did hear her mention the condos she's marketing for Ed."

I blinked. "Are you telling me Stephanie is selling the condos at the marina?" Mama nodded. "If she hated him for dumping her...I don't understand."

Mama shrugged. "Lots of money involved and those are pricey homes. I imagine she was willing to overlook her past with Ed in the name of the almighty dollar."

Now that I could see. Stephanie aspired to move in the exclusive, old money circles of Sanctuary Bay, and if her foreign sports car and designer wardrobe were any indication, she spent a ton of money.

"Good points. Add her to the suspect list, Mama."

She smiled. "Wonderful. Now how will we prove she did it?"

Oh that it were so easy. "Mama, Stephanie might not have done it. We have to follow where the clues lead us, otherwise, we're no better than Joe Brannon, picking a suspect and fitting the clues to match."

Her shoulder's sagged. "Well then, what do we do now?"

I pointed at the list she was compiling. "We figure out who else might have wanted Ed gone and then I go talk to them."

"Excuse me?" Mama looked down her nose. "*We* will talk to them."

The tilt of Mama's chin told me there was no arguing with her. I closed my eyes and prayed for strength while wondering how true the "it's five o'clock somewhere" cliché was.

Chapter Eight

In the end, the calendar saved my liver from needing a detox. It was the second Friday of the month and Mama had a standing appointment at Kitty's Kut and Kurl. No matter how much she wanted to help me find Ed's murderer, she wasn't willing to do it without a perfect coiffure.

I dropped her off at Kitty's with the promise that I would not speak to Stephanie. Not a hard vow to make because my policy had always been to avoid the snotty realtor at all costs.

Using my freedom wisely, I invited Roland and Jessica to lunch at the Country Kitchen and then placed a call to the marina in Aruba while I waited for them to arrive.

A few minutes conversation with the dockmaster's office verified what I'd suspected: Mr. and Mrs. Gregory Parrish had a slip booked for February 27th. Based upon my rudimentary knowledge of Ed's yacht, I guessed he'd planned on setting sail a few days after Valentine's Day.

That information led back to my first question. Why the false passports?

I was running possible answers over in my mind when Jessica and Roland slid onto the bench seat across from me.

"Hey, Holly, have you ordered yet?"

I smiled at Jessica and shook my head. "Nothing except for a glass of tea, though Everleigh assures me the daily special is too good to pass up."

Mentioning the cheerful server must have acted as a magical portal. "Afternoon y'all, what can I get ya?"

Everyone agreed to the meatloaf, mashed potatoes, and collard greens special, then the conversation turned to the topic uppermost in the minds of every gossip in Sanctuary Bay.

Jessica propped her elbow on the table and winked at me. "Everleigh, what's everyone saying about Ed Whitten's murder?"

I had to suppress a chuckle. Jessica knew exactly which grapevine to harvest for intel. Everleigh was the daughter Mama should have had; she collected and disseminated fodder from the gossip mill faster than you could fry an egg. Her talents came in handy.

Her cornflower blue eyes lit with excitement. "Ooh, girl, what ain't they sayin'?" She leaned closer and lowered her voice. "Most people figure he was done in because of that development on Gray's Island, but no one believes Doc Sawyer did it."

I nodded. "Good to know. I don't think Dean did it, either."

Jessica, ever the reporter looking for a story, piped up. "Why would developing the land next to the marina on Gray's Island get Ed killed?"

Everleigh snorted. "On account of them wetlands for one. Bunch o' people up in arms over Ed getting the county to let him fill them in. And then there's them condos…"

Roland looked up from his phone and frowned. "What about them? I was considering buying in; beautiful views of the sound and decent price for the location."

The chatty waitress laughed. "Yeah? Well aside from the handful they built, ain't nothin' gettin' done! Had a couple in here the other day and boy were they hot!"

Now that was interesting. Both Dean and Stephanie had challenged Ed over the condos at Gray's Island Marina. Roland's phone rang just as I was about to question Everleigh.

After he excused himself to take the call, I asked. "Everleigh, who was this couple?"

"Hmm? Oh, they were from Jersey or somewhere up north like that. Let me think..." She tapped a long pink fingernail on the table. "She had a funny name...I remember it reminded me of leprechauns."

Jessica and I exchanged glances and I mouthed the word, *leprechauns?* Had the woman been short and dressed in green?

Everleigh laughed at my comment. "Nah, it was her name...oh, I remember now. Darby! It was Darby Barrett and I don't think I got her husband's name."

After the laughter died down I managed to choke out a question to bring the conversation back to the matter at hand. "You're too much, Everleigh." I laughed again and wiped at my eyes. "So, now that we know the leprechaun's name, can you tell us what she was upset with Ed about?"

Everleigh clicked her tongue and winked. "Course I can. Her and her husband bought one of them fancy condos off Ms. Snooty Patootie Gilroy and it ain't no ways done. According to Darby, they been calling and emailing about the lack of progress and gettin' no answers so they flew down here to have it out with her." Everleigh directed a knowing look at me and Jess. "And Stephanie pointed them straight to Ed. Way Darby talked, Ms. High and Mighty was fed up with Ed, too."

My brows rose and I looked at Jessica. It was clear from her expression that she was thinking along the same lines as I was. I was about to probe for more information when Everleigh tapped the menus on the table. "I best be getting' yer orders in or y'all won't eat until midnight. Back in a few!"

"Hmm, what do you make of that?" I met Jessica's gaze. "Could Ed have been killed because of that development?"

She shrugged. "Anything's possible." She cocked a brow. "Do I take it you're looking into the murder?"

I snorted. "More like Mama and I are."

Her eyes widened. "What? Ms. Effie is trying to solve the murder?"

"Oh yes. She tried to do it on her own and was hauled in for trespassing. My hand was kinda forced after that."

Jessica's eyes danced with mirth, though she managed to hold in her laughter.

"Go ahead, I'd be laughing too, if it wasn't my mother."

She snorted and then scooted over as Roland returned to the table.

"Sorry about that. What'd I miss?"

"Nothing much, just Holly searching for clues so she can solve Ed Whitten's murder."

Roland frowned. "You've involved yourself in another crime? Is that going to take up much of your time? Because we've got to get moving on this Spruill guy."

His tone irritated me, but I pushed it aside out of consideration for what he'd been through. Losing your only son was bad enough but to then find out the official explanation for his death was false? I could understand his impatience.

Jessica was giving Roland the side-eye and the last thing I wanted was tension between our little group of investigators, so I cleared my throat and jumped in with what little I'd uncovered about Preston Spruill.

"I visited Buck Randall's dealership yesterday. I had a cover story to account for my questions, but in the end Buck saw through me but not before I got what I'd come for so, win-win!"

Ever the attorney, Roland bypassed everything I'd said and went straight for the facts. "Great! What did you learn? Did Spruill buy his expensive toys from Buck? How did he pay?"

"Slow down, Roland." I chuckled. "Yes, Spruill bought at least the motorcycle from Buck and as we suspected, he paid cash. And got a nice discount for his trouble." I added.

"So where does that leave us?" Jessica asked. "It's nice to have verification but based on Callie not finding any loan papers in her ex-husband's things, we already assumed he'd paid cash."

"Well, yes and no. The other option was that he hadn't paid for those things at all." I shook my head. "Honestly, from the moment I rolled that storage unit door up and saw Spruill's treasures my gut said he was into something illegal."

"Probably, but your instincts won't hold up in court. We need more." Roland stared out the window for a second, lost in thought.

"I agree. We need hard evidence but I'm at a loss on how to proceed." Jessica sighed. "We identified the truck captured in Roland's trail camera footage and that led us to Preston Spruill. His disappearance, coupled with the truck, and that storage unit filled with goodies makes him suspect number one in my book."

Everleigh arrived with our food so we dropped the subject. After a few bites, I set my fork down. "If Preston Spruill is a suspect, and I don't disagree with you on that, Jess, but my question is, what do we suspect him of? Are you thinking he was the one that shot Shawn and me?"

She took a sip of water before answering. "Yes? I mean, as of right now, he's the only lead we have and everything from his disappearance to his truck and the storage unit is suspicious. My question is, what happened to him?"

Roland cleared his throat. "I think we're overlooking the obvious question." Jessica and I both gave him quizzical looks. "If Spruill was the trigger man, was he acting alone or did someone hire him. And either way, why would someone want both of you dead?"

I considered everything we knew about the shooting and Spruill and then slowly nodded my head. "You have a point—a scary point. Following along that line, is someone going to come after me to finish the job?"

Jessica had been silent while Roland and I discussed the situation but one glance told me her wheels were turning. "Spit it out, Jessica. What are you thinking?"

She wrinkled her nose and shrugged. "Well, to paraphrase Roland, you're missing the obvious. Maybe you and Shawn weren't the targets."

My brows shot to my hairline and Roland choked on his tea. I recovered first. "But Jess, are you suggesting Shawn's death and my injuries were just an accident?"

"Eh...I'm thinking more like wrong place at the wrong time?"

I blinked and slumped in my seat, flabbergasted. I'd never considered...

Roland finally found his voice. "That's certainly a possibility we hadn't considered. But if that is what happened, why was Spruill on my land?"

Jessica shrugged. "That's the million-dollar question. Another is, was he alone?"

Chapter Nine

T he questions concerning the shooting and whether Spruill had been working alone were pushed from my mind minutes after I pulled out of the restaurant parking lot. The phone rang and the caller ID said it was Tate.

My track record for phone calls bearing bad news was two and zero, which made me hesitant to answer. Considering the laundry list of problems I was tasked with finding solutions for, had it been anyone but my boyfriend, I would have let it go to voicemail.

"Hey Tate, what's up?" The Colonel was twisting and turning in his seat and knocked the gear shift into neutral, distracting me from Tate's reply.

"Sorry Tate, what was that about Myrtlewood?"

"Figured you'd like an update on the bones."

My eyes widened. While I hadn't forgotten about the broken pipe and the discovery of a skeleton on our family's land, it was safe to say I'd pushed it to the back of my mind.

My grip on the wheel tightened as I asked, "Do I want to know?"

Tate laughed. "Probably not, but here it is anyway. My team removed your mystery man, it's a man by the way, and we called in a forensic anthropologist. They're still analyzing the remains but are confident the body is over two hundred years old. So, good news is your property isn't an active crime scene."

I hesitated to let out a relieved sigh. He'd said good news which meant... "What's the bad news?"

Rustling papers filled the line for a second. "Well, being that the bones are that old, and Myrtlewood was an active, slave labor plantation..."

"Oh dear. The plumbers disturbed an old cemetery?"

"Eh, it's a possibility. I took the liberty of calling an archaeologist at the state college. With Myrtlewood's history, he thinks ground penetrating radar should be brought in. If it's an isolated body that somehow ended up there you can just have the remains buried elsewhere but, if it's an old cemetery..."

"They're gonna want to document, dig, and God only knows what else."

Tate laughed. "Pretty much. What do you want to do?"

Nothing, but that wasn't an option. Whoever the man was, he deserved a decent burial and I had no problem paying for that but what Tate was describing sounded like a massive project that I had no time for.

"Tate, between looking for Ed's killer, preparing for Junior's wedding, Connie being out of town..." I sighed hard enough to rattle the phone speaker. "I can't take on a project of this size."

"Kinda figured you'd say that, so I got to thinking—"

"Oh, that's a great idea, do it!"

He laughed. "Uh, I haven't told you what I propose."

"Don't care." I laughed. "Seriously though, what do you suggest?"

"I think this is a perfect project for the newly hired curator of the Sanctuary Bay museum. Penelope is young, enthusiastic for local history, and best of all, available and interested. I've already run it by her."

Now I could breathe a sigh of relief. "Oh you are a star, Tate Sawyer, a star! Do I need to call her or…"

"Nope. I explained that you are in the middle of multiple projects at the moment and put her in touch with the professor. She promised to coordinate with him and his team and keep you updated on their progress."

Tate laughed, which made me pause. "That sounds like a great plan but, what's so funny?"

I could hear the laughter in his voice as he replied.

"Nothing, only when I said keep *you* updated, I should have said Dewey. I gave Penelope his number."

That made me laugh out loud hard enough to rouse The Colonel. "Oh goodness, Tate, you are an evil genius."

"Well, like you said. You're very busy and I figured it's his home, too. By the way, no pressure or anything but any leads on Ed's killer?"

"It's early still but I did confirm my suspicion about Aruba." I gave Tate a rundown on what I'd found and my theories.

"So he was taking a trip. How could that be tied to his death?"

"Not sure. I only found out a few minutes ago and haven't had time to look at the information as part of the bigger picture. I just finished lunch with Jessica and Roland and we didn't talk about—oh!"

"What? Is something wrong?"

"Huh? No, nothing like that. I just thought about a conversation I had with Everleigh Tucker while we were waiting for our food." I thought back to what the waitress had said about the couple from up north. A theory was taking shape but there were a few missing pieces.

"Tate? Mama said Stephanie Gilroy was arguing with Ed at the ball. I saw it kick off but took The Colonel outside and missed most of it. Did you happen to hear what they were discussing?"

Tate snorted. "Uh, yeah. Anyone seated on that side of the room probably heard. Stephanie was blaming Ed for harming her reputation. Something about the condos she's selling for him. Does that help?"

Tate confirmed what Mama thought she'd heard, and if I coupled that information with what I learned from Everleigh and added in Tate's father's issues with Ed...

"Yes it does. Mama thought she'd heard the same thing. That's three people linked to Ed's development project that are invested in some way. Add in the false passports and the trip to Aruba and what do you get?"

"Fun in the sun away from angry investors?"

I snorted. "Ah, take it a step further. Fun in the sun under an assumed name with no plans to return and answer to those angry investors."

I had to pull the phone away from my ear as Tate whistled.

"Oh boy, I really hope you're wrong about this or Dad's out a boatload of money."

I ended my call with Tate after asking him to make inquiries about any tears in Ed's clothes and then picked Mama up from the Kut and Kurl. My plan had been to drop her off at home and then spend a few hours at my office finalizing plans for my son's wedding, but after I informed her of what I'd learned from the marina in Aruba and the gossip Everleigh had provided, Mama had insisted on talking about my theory until it was time for bed.

When she started to rehash the same topic for the third time I stifled a yawn and got to my feet. "Sorry Mama, I'm beat." I nudged The Colonel awake and headed for the stairs. "We can figure out our next move tomorrow."

All I wanted to do was flop into bed and sleep like the dead, but once I'd settled The Colonel and finished my nightly routine, my brain refused to shut off.

Giving up on the idea of sleep, I let my mind roam over the facts of Ed's death for what seemed like the tenth time. He'd been murdered between 1:00 a.m. and 3:00 a.m. The marina was gated and only accessible to boat owners and people living in the condos.

Boat owners had an access code. I hadn't told Mama, but my plan was to talk to the dockmaster and see if anyone had used their gate code around the time Ed was killed.

The condo owners were another story. They had unrestricted access to the marina, but since there were only six completed units, that suspect list was short. I knew that yacht club chairman, John McGrath, lived in one of the condos, and Ed's latest girlfriend, Ava Walker, had one, too. That left four unidentified, and it was possible the dockmaster could give me their names. If not, the development's guard shack would know.

Mama was pushing for us to speak to Stephanie Gilroy first thing tomorrow, but something was telling me the hunt for Ed's killer started at the marina. The names on the fake passports kept popping into my mind.

Ed had planned to take Ava with him, going so far as to make them a married couple on the documents. Had they married in secret? It didn't seem likely, what with Ed's track record, but either way, the passport and planned trip suggested they'd had a closer relationship than his usual date 'em and leave 'em.

Yet Ava hadn't been seen since the night of the ball. I'd asked both Jessica and Everleigh and then called my former boss to double check; according to Craig, they'd wanted to speak with Ava but so far had not been able to reach her.

If she and Ed had been close enough to start new lives under assumed names, I'd have thought she would at least have called the police about Ed's death. One of those fake passports had her photo on it. Detective Brannon didn't think that worthy of further inquiry but to me, it was highly suspicious.

First thing tomorrow, I'd pay Ms. Walker a visit.

Chapter Ten

*S*omething wet is seeping into the seat of my pants. I groan and try to roll over but searing pain erupts in my leg, making me want to vomit. The pain also cleared the brain fog and I remember; I've been shot.

I've been shot and I'm lying on the dirt road in Roland Dupree's hunting camp. I manage to turn my head and come face to face with the dead eyes of Shawn Dupree. Oh God, what is happening?

I draw a shaky breath and close my eyes. I need to move. I need to get to the radio and call for help. I'm lying still, trying to summon *what little energy I have left so that I can save myself, when a twig snaps somewhere on the other side of my car.*

I listen intently. It was just a deer, Holly, focus! I'm straining to reach into the car when I hear them; someone is coming! Relief floods through me and I start to cry out that I'm here, that I need help but the voices come closer and I hold my breath as I hear, "You grab the shovel; I'll drag him over..."

My heart is pounding in my chest but I control my breathing so they think I'm dead. Who are they? Did they shoot me? Shawn? The pain in my leg is a constant throb, and I'm close to passing out.

I dig my nails into the palm of my hand, trying to stay alert. What are they doing? The drag of a shovel cutting into the earth grounds me; they're going to bury us!

Bury us and we'll never be found! I have to move; I have to find my gun—

"A stalled vehicle in the left lane has traffic snarled on 278 and construction on 95 is contributing to a slower than normal commute. Take alternate routes if you can. Coming up next, the seven-day forecast, on WRKC, Savannah, Hilton Head..."

My radio alarm broke through the nightmare, but trying to wake up was like dragging myself from the depths of the ocean.

Shaking and sticky with sweat, I flailed around and finally managed to hit the clock's snooze button, but the ensuing silence allowed my mind to wander back to the dusty road where I lay bleeding to death.

Nope, not going there! I threw off the covers and swung my legs over the side of the bed. The Colonel stumbled up from his bed and waddled over to the door, urging me to hurry if I didn't want to clean the floor at the crack of dawn. "All right, buddy, I told you to go before you went to bed."

A blast of cold air slapped me in the face as I shooed the dog outside. Frost blanketed the garden and heavy gray clouds suggested we'd have a rainy day. Hopefully it'd warm up because the last thing I needed was more fallout from a hard freeze.

I made coffee and leaned against the counter as I cautiously analyzed the nightmare. I'd been back on that dusty road in the middle of Roland's hunting camp. Most of the dream was familiar but that last part...the coffee machine sputtered and I happily pushed everything out of my mind and filled my mug.

Cradling the hot cup, I stood at the back door and absently watched The Colonel frolic in the garden as I studiously avoided thinking about what I'd seen in my dream.

Figuring that making a mental to-do list was a good way to avoid triggering my PTSD, I was compiling tasks for the day when my gaze landed on The Colonel. He was furiously digging in one of the flower beds and had made good progress; his head and shoulders were almost buried—my breath caught as a vision flashed before my eyes.

I'm sprawled in the road, playing 'possum. Voices reach me and I peer in that direction through narrowed eyes. Two men? Maybe three, I can't be sure. They are pulling something out of the bed of the truck.

Their backs are to me, I risk opening my eyes wider and see that each man is carrying one end of something. What is it? A rug? A tarp?

Moving makes my stomach roll and the sharp taste of bile burns my throat. I grit my teeth and fight against the pain. I have to see! Summoning my last bit of strength, I raise my head just as one end of the parcel they are carrying falls to the ground.

Someone shouts a curse word and the men pick it up again...what are they...I gasp as a pale, lifeless arm dangles from beneath the tarp—

"Good morning, looks like rain..."

"Oh!" I jumped and managed to slop coffee down the front of my shirt.

"Gracious, you're as jumpy as a cat in a room full of rocking chairs!" Mama rushed across the kitchen and grabbed a paper towel. "Here, wipe the floor and then give me your shirt. It'll stain if I don't soak it..." Mama's fussing trailed off as I stood upright. She cocked her head to one side and stared at me through narrowed eyes.

"Holly Marie, you're very pale and the sparkle is gone from your eyes. Are you coming down with something?"

I forced a smile and tried to look perky. "No ma'am, I didn't sleep well, that's all." I grabbed the coffee pot. "Nothing a little caffeine won't cure."

Her expression was skeptical, but after studying me for a few more seconds she nodded. "Well, if you're sure...change your shirt and make sure you put on something warm. We don't need you catching a chill."

"Yes ma'am." I called The Colonel inside and gave him his breakfast before heading upstairs. Knowing Mama's opinions on the proper appearance for public interaction, I slipped on a dressier shirt and grabbed a jacket.

Properly attired, I made my way back to the kitchen, making sure I exhibited a more energetic and carefree expression. The last thing I wanted was fussin' over my mental state.

I'd had more than enough of that in the months following the shooting. Passing my mood off as a lack of sleep had fooled Mama for now, but she was sharp and any indication the PTSD was back and she'd insist I schedule an appointment with Dr. Styles.

Not that the idea was a bad one. I considered the nightmare and its aftereffects while I wrestled The Colonel into his harness. The flashbacks and associated anxiety had dwindled to almost nothing since enough of my memory returned to indicate I had not fired my weapon, much less shot and killed Shawn Dupree.

So why had the PTSD reared its head now? A sour taste filled my mouth as I cautiously probed around the surface of the new memories. Two men, a shovel, the lifeless arm hanging from the tarp...my stomach clenched and the hand grasping The Colonel's leash started to tremble.

Stop thinking about it, Holly! Heart racing, I took shallow breaths and willed myself to calm down.

"Holly Marie? Are you ready to go? I thought we could start by talking to Stephanie and then perhaps we should—"

"Yes!" Anxious to focus on anything but the trauma, I jumped and spun around to find Mama staring at me, a suspicious look in her eyes.

Get a grip, I told myself, or you'll be badgered all day!

I cleared my throat and forced a casual smile. "We're ready and no, Mama, first on my list is talking to Ava Walker."

My mother tsked but let the matter drop in favor of catching me up on the latest gossip. I tuned out her chatter and was focused on driving and not having another flashback when something she said caught my attention.

"I'm sorry, what did you say, Mama?"

"Hmm? Oh, I was just saying that under the circumstances, I'm glad I don't have an account at Sea Islands Bank and Trust."

I frowned and tried running back through her stream of chatter to no avail. Unfortunately, in this instance, my ability to block my mother out had been successful.

"What circumstances?"

Mama huffed, as I knew she would, and scolded me for not listening. "I swear, you are just like your father. Why, he was forever asking me to repeat myself and it got to the point I suggested he have his hearing checked. But of course, there was nothing—"

"Yes ma'am, Daddy's hearing was fine." Agreeing with her and changing the subject was the only hope I had of ever finding out why she didn't want to use Sea Islands Bank. "But what is going on at the bank that makes them untrustworthy?"

She shook her head and sighed. "If you'd been listening...but no matter. I'm not saying the entire bank is not to be trusted, but I do question the integrity of any institution that keeps someone like Serena Osbourne on staff."

Serena Osbourne. I knew the name but couldn't put that to a face. Something about her was ringing a bell though. Either way my curiosity was aroused. "What did she do that has you so fired up?"

Mama rolled her eyes. "I'm not fired up; I just don't think people with questionable morals should have control of other peoples' money! But, as to what she did..." She turned in her seat. "Everyone at Kitty's was talking about it and really, Jane is to be commended. I honestly don't know what I'd have done had I been in her shoes..."

Mama continued rambling and dancing around the subject for several minutes. I managed to wait until she paused for air to demand a coherent explanation. "Mama, you still haven't told me what Serena Osbourne did!"

She pursed her lips and gave me a look, but when I held her gaze, she huffed and got to the point.

"Well, apparently, it all started when Jane Marlow's sister had twins. She already has three children, all under the age of five I might add..." She cocked her head to one side. "Pregnant that often...honestly, someone should tell her how that's happening—"

"Mama, for goodness' sake, what does Jane Marlow's sister's baby making have to do with Serena Osbourne?"

Mama's brows rose and the scold was clear in her expression. I refused to apologize. Yes, my tone was impatient and just a bit tetchy, however under the circumstances I felt it was justified.

"I was getting to that!" She shot me a dirty look. "Jane went to help her sister and while she was gone, *that woman* made a play for her husband!"

I breathed in through my nose and silently counted to five. Drama and talking behind people's backs always irritated me and having sat through several minutes of a discombobulated story about something completely irrelevant to the investigation of Ed's murder...I needed to rein in my temper before I said something I'd suffer the consequences of for the rest of the day.

When I felt in control of my tone, I cleared my throat. "That's terrible, Mama, but does it really affect her job as a banker?"

She sniffed. "It's a matter of character, Holly Marie. Serena Osbourne is the female equivalent of Ed Whitten when it comes to relationships." Her eyes widened. "In fact, If memory serves, they were an item once upon a time." She frowned.

Oh, well that was interesting. "Are you saying Serena Osbourne dated Ed Whitten?"

"Yes, I believe so but I'll have to ask around to make sure. You know, I wonder if that was what they were talking about at the ball..."

I glanced over at her as I shifted gears. "Wait, why would you think their former relationship was the topic of discussion?"

Mama shrugged. "I could be wrong, only what else could they have been talking about so intensely?"

I frowned, trying to recall seeing this exchange and came up empty. "Define intensely. Did they make a scene?"

"No, not really. I was headed to the ladies room and happened upon them as I walked down that little hallway across from the entrance to the lounge. They were standing very close and Serena was talking fast in a hushed whisper then when she saw me, she jumped back and looked guilty, if you know what I mean?"

Quiet alcove, heads together, looking guilty... Knowing Ed's reputation and from what Mama said was Serena's, I had to agree. They were probably planning an illicit assignation. Not that it was any of my business or Mama's.

I said as much and she scowled. "I'm not carryin' tales, Holly Marie. I just thought it might be pertinent to our hunt for Ed's killer." She sat up straight and shifted in her seat. "Now then what is your plan when we get to Ava's? Should I play the good cop or will you—oh no, what am I thinking no one would believe you are the nice one."

"Mama!" I laughed and shook my head. "Always nice to know how your parent sees you."

"Well, it's true Holly Marie. You can be a bit *grumpy*. And as I've always told you, you'll catch more flies with—"

"Honey than vinegar, yes ma'am." I often reminded myself of that axiom when talking to people I needed information from, not that I was gonna admit that to Mama. Since we were pulling into the marina, I changed the subject.

"Okay. Once we get to Ava's, let me do the talking. There's a knack to prying information out of a suspect."

Mama sighed and let me help her out of the truck. "That's fine, dear. Though it isn't as if I don't have that skill set."

I blinked and bit back a laugh because the reigning queen of the Sanctuary Bay gossip mill was absolutely right.

Chapter Eleven

I pounded on Ava's door for the third time and hollered her name for good measure, but there was no reply, not so much as a sound came from inside. I was about to give it up for a lost cause when John McGrath called out from the condo across the courtyard.

"I don't think she's home!"

While appreciated, I'd already guessed as much. I waved an acknowledgment and John made his way over to us. "Mornin'

Holly." He nodded to Mama. "Ms. Effie. Hope y'all were comfortable in the apartment the other night."

"Yes indeed. Thank you again, John." Mama shuddered. "Wonderful party and Holly's decorations were lovely, but I dreaded sleeping in the ballroom."

John grinned. "Absolutely! Seemed like everyone enjoyed themselves, until the ice set in. Shame about Ed though." He looked at me. "Hear you found him."

"Yes, unfortunately." I tipped my head toward Ava's door. "I wanted to check on Ava. I called her office and they haven't heard from her since the beginning of the week. Any idea where she is?"

John shook his head. "No, I haven't seen her since the ball." He looked toward Ava's condo and frowned. "In fact, I haven't noticed any lights on or anything...you reckon' she's okay?"

"Eh...I'm beginning to wonder..." She'd been with Ed the night of the ball and now both her employer and her neighbor were claiming not to have heard from her. My cop radar was clanging. "Let's take a closer look."

John and Mama trailed after me as The Colonel and I walked back to the front door. Another round of knocking and hollering without results sent me around the side of the house.

"What are you doing?" Mama whined. "It's starting to drizzle and the forecast said it might freeze."

Ignoring her, I stood on tiptoe and tried to peer into a window. The blinds were drawn so I continued to the back of the house. Mama trailed after me, complaining all the way.

This was why I preferred to work alone! I sighed. "Mama, go back to the truck and wait." Commanding The Colonel to sit and stay, I crossed the small porch and tried the doorknob. "I just want to check—hey, the door is unlocked!"

Mama quieted as I turned the knob and pushed the door open. "Ava? It's Holly Daye. Are you all right?"

I stepped over the threshold and waited for a reply my gut said wasn't coming. The house was eerily still.

"Uh, should we be doing this? I mean, maybe we should call the cops..."

My instincts were screaming something was wrong and I didn't disagree with John. I should step back and call the police and I would, just as soon as I took a look around.

"John, you and Mama stay out here. Mama, make sure The Colonel doesn't get loose." Expecting compliance with my commands, I walked through the kitchen, listening, but not expecting any reaction to my entrance.

The kitchen was all modern and sleek. White cabinets, black marble countertops, stainless steel appliances...everything was neat, tidy, and shining like a new penny, except for an overturned bar stool and spots of something crusted on the floor.

I bent and examined them. My unscientific opinion said they were drops of blood. The hair on the back of my neck rose and a sour taste flooded my mouth.

Careful not to touch anything, I moved into the combination living and dining room. A wall of built-in bookcases lined one wall and the contents were scattered on the floor. A potted ficus lay on it's side, and the cabinet doors were all open.

This room had been searched. By whom and what they were looking for I couldn't say, but someone had definitely been frantically looking for something. I gulped and moved to the hallway.

Not expecting a reply, I still called Ava's name as I climbed the stairs and started opening doors.

The first room to the left of the stairs, set up as an office, was empty and showed similar signs of having been searched. I crossed the landing to what I assumed was the main bedroom and knocked. When I got no reply, I nudged the door open and gasped.

The bed skirt was ripped and all of the linens were in a heap by the French doors. The dresser drawers were opened and clothes were strewn across the room, and the bedside lamps were on the floor.

I was backing out of the room when a flash of black against the stark white carpet caught my eye. It was the ballgown Ava had worn. It was a white sheath dress that Mama had exclaimed was someone or other designer's...a dress costing an arm and a leg usually wasn't treated so shabbily.

The dress was a few feet away from the entrance to the bathroom and beside it were more drops of what I now was convinced was blood. I grabbed a hand towel from the bathroom and used it to cover my hand as I smoothed the dress out.

Splotches of blood marred the neckline and dripped down the front, a few pearls that matched those on the dress were glistening on the carpet. My eyes widened as I glanced further down the dress.

The splashes of black that had drawn me to the gown were bows. I'd forgotten that detail. Ava's designer gown was white with black bows. Three to be exact.

Perfectly aligned down the dress from the waist to the knee, the middle bow was missing one end. I couldn't prove it one hundred percent, but my gut said Ava had been on the dock when Ed was killed.

She must have caught her dress on the rough wooden piling but had it happened as she approached the yacht or when she ran away? If it was the latter, was she running in fear of what she'd seen happen to Ed or was she running from the crime she'd just committed?

I backed out of the room and dialed 911 as I joined Mama and John on the back porch. Ava killing Ed would wrap everything up with a neat little bow, but that scenario didn't jive with the state of her house or the blood. I'd paid Ava a visit in hopes of getting answers. I was leaving with nothing but more questions.

Chapter Twelve

For the second time in under an hour I found myself shaking my head and saying, "I don't know."

Mama sighed and clucked her tongue but Tate was working off his frustration by pacing a hole in my carpet. He spun around and slapped his hand down on the mantel.

"Well what do you know?" He dragged a hand through his hair and winced when I gave him a censorious look. "I'm sorry. It's just...we have nothing and Dad is sitting in a jail cell!"

Blowing out a breath, I flopped onto the couch and considered Dr. Sawyer's situation. He was scheduled for arraignment in three days and his attorney wasn't confident he could get a judge to set bail.

Knowing the older man was cooped up in a cell just added pressure I didn't need. Doctor Sawyer had been a fixture in Sanctuary Bay my whole life and his reputation among the citizens should hold weight with the judge. If I could get some character witnesses along with the flimsy evidence, it might be enough for a judge to grant bail.

Tate and Mama were both distraught over Dean's arrest and grasping at any straw for ways to save him. I'd quietly seek some testimonials for Dean and then inform Mama and Tate of my plan. Making a mental list of people I thought might vouch for the good doctor, I moved on to the problem of finding the real killer of Ed Whitten, not that I had any good prospects in that department.

We'd been forced to stay on the scene while the police conducted another search of Ava's home and it had taken hours. I was exhausted and no closer to solving Ed's murder, but there'd be no peace until I had a solid lead.

I sighed and got down to business. "Okay, they've opened a missing person's case on Ava. I talked with Craig and he said Brannon isn't suspecting her of the murder, though he has no other theory for what's happened to her." I looked at Tate and Mama. "We need background on Ava. Is she capable of killing Ed? If so, why? If not, then where is she? Problem is, I've no idea how to get that information."

Mama cleared her throat. "I might be able to help."

"How so, Mama?"

"Well, last year Bernice Ziggler finally got that cheapskate husband of hers to build a sunroom and she managed to wring enough money out of him to hire a decorator."

My brows rose. "And she used Ava?"

Mama nodded. "I think so. I know it was someone with Signature Interiors anyway. If you think it'll help, I'll call Bernice first thing in the morning."

"Great idea Mama! If it was Ava, ask Ms. Bernice what she knows about her. If it wasn't, maybe we can talk to whoever did the job. Hopefully, one of her colleagues knows Ava well enough to answer some questions."

"Mmm, it's possible. While we were waiting for the police to let us leave I called Lou Lou and between us, we can't recall Ava having any family ties in Sanctuary Bay."

That tracked with what little I knew of the woman. To my knowledge, she hadn't been in Sanctuary Bay very long but I didn't make it a habit to know everyone and their business, like Mama and the mayor did.

"All right, tomorrow see what you can find out about Ava's past while I talk to Stephanie Gilroy and that couple from up north that bought a condo. After that, I'm out of ideas so we need to think about other possible suspects."

I sighed as Mama and Tate gave me blank looks. "Come on, think. Who hated Ed enough to kill him and also had access to the marina?"

"John Mcgrath lives there, but I don't know of any reason he'd want to kill Ed." Tate shrugged. "They were good friends in high school and Ed hired him as the chairman of his yacht club."

I nodded. "Yeah, I don't see John as a suspect, but who else has a condo or a boat docked at the marina? Ava of course, but right now that's a dead end." Everyone fell silent, leaving me to determine our next course of action. "Okay, we need a list of people with boats at the marina and the owners of the other condos. Best way to get that information is the dockmaster, unless y'all have a better idea?"

None was forthcoming so I made a mental note to visit the marina office. "Let's go over what we know or suspect. One, the killer could have been motivated to kill Ed over his treatment of them while dating, or it could have been related to the questionable business practices concerning the condos and marina. Two, we know the killer had to be someone with access to the gated marina, which means a boat owner or one of the condo residents." I started to move to number three when Tate cleared his throat.

"Um, there might be another motive. I was at the Split Bean this morning and heard some chatter about the Gray's Island protestors. You know they hired a lawyer to stop Ed, right?"

I quirked a brow. "No, I didn't know that! We need to find out which residents are leading the charge and what legal eagle they hired."

Tate nodded. "I can answer part of that. Felicity Simms is the one that organized her neighbors and I assume she also hired the attorney."

I closed my eyes and winced. Of all people, it just had to be Felicity. She'd been a suspect in the murder of Brianna Bellamy last Christmas and hadn't taken kindly to my questions. Finding out I'd put her on another suspect list was going to go over like a lead balloon.

I shook my head and accepted my fate, but at this rate, I was going to be voted most hated citizen of Noble County.

Chapter Thirteen

Stephanie's office opened in thirty minutes, which left me plenty of time to think, unfortunately.

After Tate left, I'd fallen into bed and expected to sleep like the dead but I'd barely closed my eyes when the nightmares began. Once again I was reliving the night of the shooting, with the time I lay bleeding out repeating like a broken record until it skipped to the lifeless arm poking out of a tarp being carried by two shadowy figures.

Twice I'd awakened in a cold sweat. The third time I tried to get a little more shut-eye, but by that point I was so afraid of what I might dream that I tossed and turned until my alarm went off.

I walked The Colonel along Prince Street and tried to keep my mind focused on the coming discussion with the snotty realtor. My brain had other ideas and no matter what I did, the remnants of what I'd dreamed kept popping into the forefront of my thoughts.

Frustrated and tired of being a coward, I decided to face the contents of the nightmare head-on. If I could remain emotionally detached, perhaps I could figure out why the PTSD had returned. For now, I'd push all thoughts of the nightmare to the back of my mind; no way was I risking a panic attack in public!

The Colonel slowed his pace to a crawl, a sure signal he was ready to flop. Since the weather was still unseasonably cold, I set off toward Bay Street. Maybe all I needed was a strong cup of coffee and one of Bill's chocolate croissants.

Choosing a table by the windows that overlooked Bay Street, I'd just taken a cautious sip of the scalding hot coffee when Felicity Simms walked in.

Talking to her was on my to-do list, and even though I dreaded the discussion and would have preferred drinking my coffee in peace, I forced myself to approach her; no sense delaying the inevitable.

She was standing to the side of the counter, waiting for her order. I got within hearing range and said, "Felicity."

She spun around and for a split second, her eyes showed irritation before a polite mask slid onto her face.

"Holly, nice to see you." The stiff way she held her shoulders made a lie of that statement. "How's Ms. Effie?"

The hostility I'd anticipated was evident so I made a quick decision. No matter the circumstantial evidence, I didn't think Felicity had killed Ed. Better to make her an ally than keep an enemy.

Dawning a concerned expression, I set about getting back into Felicity's good graces. "Mama's well, thanks for asking." I sighed. "Well, except for worrying about Doc Sawyer. To tell the truth, I'm concerned about her. His arrest has been a terrible shock and the Lord only knows how she'll take it if he should be convicted."

Felicity's eyes widened. "Gracious! Do you think that's a possibility?"

I shrugged. "If I can't figure out who really did it, yes."

"Oh, so you're looking into the murder. I should have known." She muttered under her breath.

I pretended not to hear the snarky remark. "Yes, I am. I didn't want to interfere with police matters but you know what Joe Brannon is like and then Mama and Tate were so upset..." I shook my head. "I didn't feel like I had much choice."

My ploy seemed to be working as Felicity unbent a little. Her expression was sympathetic as she replied.

"It's good of you to take on such a responsibility, and you're very good at it! We were all shocked to find out who killed that little witch, Brianna, God rest her soul. I'm sure you'll figure out who killed Ed. You have quite a track record!" She flashed an encouraging smile and turned to pick up her drink.

"Thank you, I wish I had your confidence." I cast my gaze downward and slumped my shoulders, hoping to appear forlorn and pitiful. "There's very little to go on and what leads I have seem to be dead ends."

She tsked. "Oh my, that's too bad. I'm going to grab a table. Join me?" She started toward the seating area and I trooped along.

We settled at the table and Felicity studied my forlorn expression for a second before patting my hand. "You poor thing. You've taken on quite a load. If there's anything I can do to help, you have only to ask."

I glanced at her from beneath my lashes and bit back a grin. Her words were full of empathy, but there was also a spark in Felicity's eyes I'd seen many times in my mother's; it was the look of someone eager to be taken into someone's confidence and I was ready to oblige. I'd dangled the bait, now it was time to set the hook and reel her in.

"Oh, Felicity that's very kind, but I can't think..." I pretended to consider her offer and then feigned surprise. "Oh! Now that I think of it, perhaps you might know, seeing as you live on Gray's Island."

Eagerness shown from her eyes. "I'm happy to help if I can." She shuddered. "Though I hope the guilty person isn't an islander. Imagine having two murderers in our little community!"

I opted not to comment on the murder of Brianna Bellamy last Christmas that had dragged me, my assistant, and several residents of the island into a criminal investigation. "Yes, what are the odds? But I'm afraid it might be true. The police think Ed might have been killed over the marina development. You know, on account of the protestors? And I've heard they now plan to sue. Though no one seems to know which attorney is handling the case."

"What?" She rolled her eyes. "That's ridiculous. We are all very unhappy with the destruction of the wetlands and the removal of several live oaks, but none of us would kill to stop it!"

"Us?" I played dumb. "Are you part of the group that's protesting?"

"Part? Why I went door to door getting my neighbors to support the injunction. I gathered more than five hundred signatures and you know there are only 839 full-time residents on our island."

My lips twitched at Felicity tooting her own horn, but I managed to look suitably impressed. "That's wonderful! You're so civic-minded. We are lucky to have you. But you said you organized a petition to get an injunction. I don't understand. If you had that much support, how did Ed manage to get county approval?"

She sniffed. "Commissioner Gerald Vandershall and his good friend J.T. Minton. That's how." She scowled. "Those two are thick as thieves. And of course it's Minton's company doing the construction." She added archly.

I frowned, recalling the signs and equipment scattered around the building site. "The signs I saw were for Bethel Construction. I figured they were a firm out of Charleston."

Felicity shook her head. "You thought wrong. First thing Gabriella Crestfield did after we put her on retainer was look into Bethel." She smirked. "Guess who owns it?"

My jaw dropped. "Minton?"

She tipped her head. "Right in one. Now what does that tell you?"

A lot. If Felicity was correct about Minton having the construction contract, he earned a spot near the top of my suspect list.

J.T. was well-known and well-liked throughout the county, but I could not be counted as one of his fans. Yes, he was community minded and donated to all the *things,* but something about him set my cop alarm off. He was too smooth, too friendly, just *too* much.

CoaStyle and Glitter and Garland were located in one of Minton's most ambitious developments, and the Canary Wharf project was by no means finished. The ground floor units were, but he'd touted the project as a condo/retail community and two years into the construction, only five shops were finished and leased.

Come to think of it, that was a heck of a lot like Ed Whitten's development...

Before my forced retirement, I'd broken up a fight between Minton and Mr. Archelaus, the old man that owed Sea Islands Gift Shop. At the time, I'd been more interested in keeping the two senior citizens from pummeling each other, but thinking back, I recalled Mr. Archelaus was angry over the lack of progress, and he'd said something about his money before I'd pulled him away.

Could that incident have any bearing on—

"Does that help, Holly?"

I blinked and focused on Felicity, though my mind was still mulling over what I'd learned about J.T. "Hmm? Oh, yes it does, very much so!" I considered what she'd told me and how it fit into the picture I was forming. "I hate to say it, but with so many people unhappy over Ed's development, maybe one of them took things a little too far."

Felicity snorted. "That, or his playboy ways caught up with him." She shrugged and got to her feet. "Either way, good riddance to bad rubbish." She tossed her cup into the trashcan and waved. "I've got to run. Let me know if I can help with anything else."

Felicity's comment was a little harsh, but I was hard pressed to disagree. Between his Gray's Island neighbors and the string of women he'd played fast and loose with, Ed Whitten had made a lot of enemies in Sanctuary Bay.

Chapter Fourteen

T he Colonel and I were headed for the Sea Islands Realty office when my phone rang. After several minutes listening to Mama tell me some convoluted story involving Bernice Ziggler and her new sunroom I managed to interrupt and force her to get to the point.

A burst of air rattled the speaker as Mama huffed. "I wish you'd stop interrupting me. It breaks my concentration and I always say—"

"Mama, I'm almost to Stephanie's office. Can I call you later?"

"No. That's why I'm calling!" She mumbled something and then returned to the line. "I've just found a parking space and will be there in a minute. Wait for me!"

The line went dead, preventing any argument so I twiddled my thumbs and waited like the dutiful, or henpecked, daughter I was.

"There, now let me tell you what Bernice said about Ava before we interrogate Stephanie."

My brows shot up at the word interrogate, but I let Mama have her way. The path of least resistance was less stressful where my mother was concerned.

"It was as I thought. Ava designed Bernice's sunroom, and it is truly lovely. You'll have to come visit with me sometime." She frowned. "That row of windows looking out over the garden provides a wonderful view, but if we do what we're talking about and close in the back porch I don't think I'll have the windows go all the way to the floor. Ethyl has made such a mess—"

"Ethyl? I thought Ava did the decorating." I was completely lost.

She rolled her eyes. "She did! Ethyl is Bernice's pug and as I was trying to say, that dog of yours would slobber all over floor to ceiling windows so I think we'll go with—"

"Mama!" Oh, how to tell one's mother to fish or cut bait! I drew a deep breath and willed myself to speak in a respectful tone. "It's getting late. Please tell me what you learned about Ava Walker so we can go talk to Stephanie."

Mama pursed her lips. "I was getting to that! It seems that Ava grew up in Aiken. She was raised by her father. But her mother lived here for a while."

I frowned. "Um, that's interesting but how does that help us?"

Mama's eyes narrowed. "I'm not sure that it does, though Bernice seemed to recall that there was some gossip about the woman and Ed Whitten."

"What?" My mind whirled. "Are you telling me that Ava Walker's mother and Ed Whitten were involved?"

Mama shrugged. "That's what Bernice thought, but I haven't had time to look into it. Do you think it's important?"

I blinked away my surprise and considered the new piece to the puzzle that was Ed's death. "Maybe? Either way, can you confirm the two were an item?"

Mama nodded. "Of course, dear. I'll make some phone calls this afternoon."

My mother's intel network rivaled the NSA. I had no doubt she'd get the story before the day ended. "Great. Now let's pay Ms. Gilroy a visit."

Biting my tongue, I let Mama continue to chat with Stephanie as I considered what little I knew about Ed Whitten and his enemies. According to Felicity Simms, J. T. Minton owned the construction company that had the Gray's Island Marina contract.

If what I suspected was true of Ed's intentions with the fake passports, Minton would have a lot to lose. I'd definitely be talking to him. Then there was the Ava Walker and her mother angle. I'd have to wait for Mama to work her network, but if it was true that Ava's mother and Ed had been an item, why would Ava have been dating Ed?

It made no sense unless she hadn't been aware of that history. Conversely, maybe she had known and dating Ed had been a ruse? Things were getting complicated. I shook my head and tried to follow Mama and Stephanie's conversation.

"I'm definitely interested in any project that promotes young women in business, Ms. Effie. Please let me know when the Women's Institute meets again." Stephanie met my gaze, a stiff but polite smile on her face. "It was nice talking to y'all, but if that's all, I have an appointment in thirty minutes."

Mama had softened her up and I was up to bat. Seeing no reason to pretend Stephanie and I were friends, I chose to come out swinging.

"I wanted to ask you about your relationship with Ed Whitten."

She stiffened, though her polite mask remained in place as her glance flitted between me and Mama. "Relationship?" Her laugh was forced. "I really don't see how that is any of your business."

I shrugged and ignored the dark look Mama shot me. "In the scheme of things, it's not, unless you killed him for dumping you. I'm looking into his death and you were arguing with him at the Valentine's Day ball."

"He didn't dump me, it was mutual." She huffed and rolled her eyes. And a tiff at the party makes me a suspect?"

"You tell me."

The air was filled with tension. From the corner of my eye I could see Mama fidgeting with the strap of her pocket book. Stephanie showed no signs of unease but there was a cold look in her eyes.

Gazes locked, we stared for several seconds before Stephanie snorted and rolled her eyes. "This is ridiculous. You no longer work for the sheriff's department, what gives you the right—"

"You talk to me, or I tell Brannon about the very public fight between you and Ed hours before he died." I shrugged. "If you're questioned by the police, it'll be all over town by tomorrow morning. Not sure how potential clients will react, but it's your funeral."

Her brows shot to her hair line. "Are you threatening me?"

The polite mask fell, just as I'd intended. A defensive suspect was a vulnerable suspect.

I kept my expression casual and unconcerned. "Not a threat. You can avoid that scenario by answering my questions."

She scowled at me and we were back to another silent stare off, but when I didn't budge, Stephanie huffed and tossed her ink pen onto the desk in disgust. "Fine. What do you want to know?"

I smiled like the cat that got the cream. "Where were you between 1:00 a.m. and 3:00 a.m. the night of the ball?"

She rolled her eyes. "Where any sane person was, home in bed."

"Alone?"

Her eyes widened. "What's that supposed to mean?"

"Nothing, I just wondered if anyone could corroborate."

Her lip curled. "As it happens, there is. Mama is staying with me while her kitchen is being remodeled."

Beside me Mama stiffened. Ruby Gilroy. Yeah, I was gonna take Stephanie at her word because the last thing I needed was for my mother to come face to face with her rival.

"Okay." I nodded. "You argued with Ed at the ball though. Care to tell me why?"

She rolled her eyes. "Not really, but if it will get you out of my office..." She sighed. "If you must know, Ed was cutting me in for a percentage of sales. I sold the six condos that are completed and another ten that aren't. The deal we made was six percent of the sale price at closing. For the lots I sold, if construction runs over ninety days, I get half my total commission with the rest due at closing."

"Good deal. So what's the problem?"

Stephanie snorted. "The problem is that, as of now, I am owed roughly $350,000, and that is just for the completed homes. I should have been paid at closing but Ed claimed his office forgot to cut the checks. I called every day for over a month, and he finally paid me ten thousand, but that's a far cry from what I'm owed. He still hasn't responded to my request for the three percent because those other condos aren't finished!"

Stephanie fairly vibrated with anger. That suited me fine because an angry suspect was more likely to let something slip, but Mama's empathy got in the way.

Before I could stop her, she stepped closer and patted Stephanie's shoulder. "That's outrageous! You have every right to be angry, Stephanie." She shook her head and tsked. "That Ed was conning everyone. Why, Dean put a sizable amount down on one of those condos, and when he saw no work being done and started calling Ed, he got the same runaround."

I held my breath, hoping Mama's actions hadn't shut the conversation down, but to my shock, Stephanie lapped up the sympathy.

"He isn't the only angry homeowner, Ms. Effie. I've been cussed out by several clients and one has threatened to report me to the realty board."

"Was one of them the couple from Jersey?"

"I'm not even gonna ask how you know that." She snorted and mumbled something about gossiping old biddies. "As it happens, the Barretts are furious that their home isn't even close to being finished, and they are from Boston, not New Jersey."

I shrugged. Everleigh had been right about the most important parts. "So what are they planning to do? Did they confront Ed?"

She shook her head. "I told you they are blaming me, and no, Ed didn't take their calls either. I begged for a little more time and promised to get answers from Ed. With the ice storm forecasted, they were afraid of getting stranded and took an early flight out."

She looked at me and scowled. "I'd had it with Ed and his excuses, but I didn't kill him. That would have been cutting my nose off to spite my face. I want to get paid!"

My brow furrowed as I considered her statement. "Stephanie, are you saying now that Ed is dead, you aren't going to get what you're owed?"

She sighed and slumped in her chair. "It looks that way." Her gaze bounced around for a second then she looked back at me and lowered her voice. "I shouldn't tell you this, but the bank is investigating Ed's account. Seems most of the eight million he was holding in escrow is"—she made an air quotes motion—"unaccounted for."

"I knew it!" Mama shot me a knowing look. "Didn't I tell you something was rotten at that bank? Never do business where they hire people with questionable morals, Holly Marie."

I was about to reply but Stephanie beat me to it.

"What do you mean, Ms. Effie? Are you suggesting someone at the bank stole the money?"

Mama started to answer but I shot her a look and shook my head. "No. Mama is referring to some gossip about one of the bank employees flirting with a married man. It has nothing to do with this situation."

Stephanie snorted. "Oh, you mean Serena Osbourne." She waved her hand. "I don't know why everyone is shocked. Serena has always played the field. Probably why she and Ed couldn't make it work. Neither is trustworthy."

So I'd heard, repeatedly. However, I had to stifle a laugh because Stephanie didn't have a stellar reputation when it came to men, either. But, armed with more information, I was fast coming to the conclusion that Ed's business dealings and not his love life had gotten him killed.

All of the home buyer complaints, the angry residents of Gray's Island, and now problems with the escrow account. Trouble with that line of thinking was, when had the killer found out about the missing money?

"Stephanie, when did you find out there was a problem with the escrow account?"

"Hmm? Oh, this morning when I went to Royal Ventures and demanded they cut me a check. Took some doing, but I finally got the acting CEO to see me. He admitted there were some *irregularities* with the account and he was unable to access the funds at the moment." She rolled her eyes. "In other words, I'm up a creek without a paddle."

I nodded and mulled over what I'd learned. The escrow account was all but empty, Ed had fake passports and a slip reserved at a marina in Aruba. Everything pointed to him embezzling the money and heading for the hills. That had to be why he was killed. Trouble was, which of the many angry people he'd conned had done it?

"So the other officers at Royal Ventures just found out the money was missing?"

"From what I gathered. The whole office is in an uproar. Phones were ringing off the hook, people running back and forth between desks and filing cabinets. They all looked shell-shocked."

"By chance, did you talk to the bank manager?"

She shook her head. "No, wouldn't do any good. The commercial department handled Ed's business and Serena Osbourne was the liaison for the account. She and I are not on good terms, so I've decided to put all of this into my attorney's hands."

"That's the best thing you can do, dear. Let the lawyers fight it out." Mama tapped her fingernails on the desk. "Do you girls think Ed was killed because someone found out he'd stolen all of that money?"

Preferring not to discuss the matter with Stephanie, I simply shrugged, but the realtor had no such qualms.

"Makes sense. I mean, it's doubtful any of those buyers will end up with a completed home, and then there's the contractors. I haven't checked, but I'll bet none of them have been paid, either."

I hated to admit it, but she was right. I needed to talk to J.T. Minton. I'd seen pallets of materials near the foundations poured for the next phase of the build. The contractor would have paid for them, and on top of that outlay of cash, they'd also have paid wages.

The missing escrow funds opened up a can of worms. I now had more suspects and no easy answers.

Chapter Fifteen

After talking with Stephanie, I was a woman on a mission. Mama wanted to grab lunch but I coaxed her into another stop: J.T. Minton's office.

Mama and I arrived at Coastal Construction just in time. J.T. was on his way out, but I, or rather Mama, coaxed him into giving us a few minutes of his time.

He ushered us into his office and motioned for us to sit in the chairs opposite his desk. "Now then..." He slid into his chair and leaned back, the picture of a relaxed executive. "What can I do for you ladies?"

Thick and wavy salt-and-pepper hair, a perpetual tan, and perfectly straight, white teeth...the man was just too smooth and he made my skin crawl.

Wanting to get in and get out, I was about to bluntly ask him where he was during the time of Ed's murder and why he'd formed a new company to do the marina job when Mama reached over and squeezed my leg in a gentle warning I'd experienced dozens of times as a child sitting in a church pew.

I frowned in her direction, but Mama, bright smile firmly in place, was looking at J.T.

"Thank you for seeing us J.T., you're always such a gentle-men. Why my Charles always said you were the salt of the earth and of course—"

"I appreciate that, Ms. Effie, but I do have to leave shortly. How can I be of assistance?"

Mama's smile never faltered and she kept her breezy tone as she invented a need for donations to a raffle her women's group was holding. At least I assumed it was fictitious. Either way, she was charming Minton and I was content to watch her work.

"So you see, all of the funds will go toward a scholarship for a young lady that shows promise as a future business leader. I just knew you'd appreciate the cause, seeing as how you're a self-made man."

J.T.'s smile widened. "You flatter me, dear lady, and of course I'm happy to donate to such a worthy cause. I can't think of anything we have that would work as a raffle item so why don't I just write you a check?" He reached out and tapped a button on the desk phone. When his secretary answered he glanced at Mama. "Will a thousand do, Ms. Effie?"

My brows rose at the sum he was willing to give away, but Mama, bless her heart, took it as her due. "Oh, we can certainly make do with that, J.T." She tsked and shook her head. "Your generosity is so refreshing. You know some of our local businessmen are penny pinchers. Why, take Ed Whitten, may he rest in peace."

J.T. smiled and quirked a brow. "Ed wasn't willing to donate?"

Mama shook her head. "No, no. He did give us a hundred dollars, and of course we're grateful for any and all donations, however, with an empire like Ed's one would think he could be a little more generous." Her smile faded as she adopted a concerned expression. "Of course, rumor has it Ed was in some financial difficulties, poor man."

J.T. stiffened when Mama mentioned Ed's financial difficulties and I watched him closely as she continued.

Sotto voce, Mama leaned forward. "A little bird told me the Royal Ventures offices are in chaos today." She widened her eyes and tipped her head to one side. "Apparently, there is quite a lot of money missing from that marina project account."

J.T. shot upright like he'd been poked with a cattle prod. "What? Where did you hear this?"

Mama shrugged and smiled serenely. "Oh, you know here and there, but I was just talking to Stephanie Gilroy. You know she was handling the marketing and sales for Ed?" J.T. nodded. "Well, she's owed a lot of money and it doesn't look as if she'll see a dime!"

J.T. paled and his trademark cool slipped as he stammered an excuse to cut their chat short. "I...I'm sorry Ms. Effie, but I really must dash..." He rose and held the door open with a hand that was trembling slightly. "You...uh...can wait out here while Mary gets your check or leave your um...address and she'll put it in the mail."

"Oh, that's too bad, but I know how busy you are." Mama patted his arm as she walked through the door. "Now you simply must come by the house when you can chat awhile longer. Come along, Holly Marie, let the man run his business."

I fought the laugh begging to be released and meekly followed Mama, but as I passed J.T. I stopped and casually asked. "For the record, mind telling me where you were between 1:00 a.m. and 3:00 a.m. the morning after the ball?"

His eyes widened and he stammered. "Wh-what? Why would you..." His gaze darted between me and my angelic looking mother before his eyes widened.

It was fun watching realization dawn. Mr. Smooth Operator had been played, so I drove the stake in a little deeper. "I'm looking into the murder of Ed Whitten and one of those little birds Mama mentioned says you have the marina construction contract under a new company name. It's interesting that you opened a new company and kept it secret...but no matter. With the escrow account funds missing, you'll be out a lot of money. That's a powerful motive..."

His lip curled and for a second hate shimmered in his eyes, then he blinked and the friendly mask fell back into place.

He chuckled. "Sugah, it's true one of my companies won the contract to build Ed's waterfront complex, but I assure you I had no reason to want the man dead." His tone was jovial but the look in his eyes suggested he wished to see me in a dark and fiery pit. "I don't owe you an answer nor an explanation, but in the spirit of civic duty I'll tell you that I was at home, as any sane person would be at that time of the morning, not to mention the wretched weather."

I started to speak but he talked over me. "And before you ask, yes my housekeeper can vouch for me. The garage remote wasn't working and I didn't have the front door key. Poor woman had to let me in."

His stare was hard and unforgiving, but the megawatt smile never faltered as he ushered me to the door. He nodded politely and bid Mama a good day, but as I walked past his hand wrapped around my arm, stopping me in my tracks.

Speaking through clenched teeth, he whispered. "Not a good idea to go around accusing folks of horrendous crimes, Ms. Daye." He released me and opened the outer door. "I'd think after your brush with death you'd be a might more careful where you tread."

Chapter Sixteen

Much to my disgust, Minton's parting shot had hit its mark. My stomach was in knots and no matter how hard I tried to hide my unease, it must have shown on my face because Mama peppered me with questions about my health until I dropped her at home.

While Mama had been helpful during the interviews with Stephanie and Minton, I was grateful her duties as an officer of the garden club would take up the rest of the evening.

After having my chain rattled by J.T., I needed a bit of peace and quiet. I also needed to figure out who had killed Ed Whitten and to accomplish that, I needed to think.

A walk along the waterfront was the perfect way to clear my head. After letting The Colonel sniff and snort every blade of grass, I found an unoccupied swing and settled back to watch the boats go by.

I took a few minutes to simply exist, but the wind was picking up and temperatures were falling fast; time to get my brain in gear. Pulling the suspect list from my pocket, I considered the case.

Mama and I had started with the premise that a jilted lover could have been the motivation for Ed's murder. To that end, we'd put Stephanie Gilroy in the suspect column and a question mark for the woman Mama couldn't remember.

While I was thinking about it, I pulled out my phone and sent Mama a text. Ms. Lou Lou and Maybelle were part of the garden club, and along with the other ladies of her gossip circle, someone was bound to recall the name of Ed's other angry ex.

Not expecting an immediate reply, I moved on to what I'd learned from Stephanie. The missing escrow money hadn't surprised me. Finding the forged passports and then the reservation for a marina in Aruba had already lead me to believe Ed was planning a one-way trip, and the missing money just solidified my theory.

Having proof he'd embezzled did open up more suspects and that led me to the biggest takeaway from my chat with Stephanie. J.T. Minton was the builder for Ed's project and he'd secretly formed a new company to do it.

I couldn't begin to guess why he'd felt the need to keep his involvement quiet, but in the scheme of things, it was irrelevant. Despite my conviction that Ed's embezzlement had gotten him killed, J.T. had to be cleared as a suspect. Alibi aside, there'd been no faking his shock when Mama informed him the escrow account was empty.

However, that didn't mean the motive wasn't valid. Trouble was, who else both knew the account was empty and would have suffered because of it?

Aside from the construction company, Ed owed Stephanie money for marketing and sales. I assumed the architect would have been paid before building began which just left me with the angry home buyers.

Dr. Sawyer was angry that work hadn't even begun on his property but I knew he wasn't capable of murder. The couple from Boston were also displeased, but they'd agreed to let the realtor handle it and had returned home. That needed to be verified but they wouldn't have had access to the marina so I moved it down on my priority list.

A gust of wind blew in off the water, making me shiver. The sun was fading fast and with it, temperatures were falling. I whistled for The Colonel, and as we made our way to the truck I continued to mull over the murder of Ed Whitten.

An angry woman intent on revenge for being used and discarded was still a possibility, but the missing escrow was flashing in my head like a neon sign. I had exhausted the list of people who were in line to receive portions of that money in exchange for services, but maybe I was looking at the situation the wrong way.

I bundled The Colonel into the truck and cranked the heater as my mind followed along the new path. Eight million was a lot of money and none had been found on the yacht. Ed was planning to run away on that yacht so it made sense he'd have the cash with him. So where was it—oh! My eyes widened as my memory kicked in.

The state of Ava Walker's house suggested it had been thoroughly searched. At the time, I'd brushed it aside in my concern for her, but...what if the killer was looking for the money? The more I considered it, the more I was convinced that was the case. However, if the killer had searched Ava's place, it meant I now had zero suspects.

Frustrated and in no mood to go home and listen to Mama badger me about saving Dean, I took a left out of the park. Driving always cleared my head so I'd take the scenic route. For lack of a better idea, I decided to go to Gray's Island and talk to the security guards and hopefully, the dockmaster.

I'd just turned onto the highway that crossed the marsh when my phone rang. Turning on the speaker, I set the phone onto the dashboard and hollered, "Hey Jess, what's up?"

"Hi, um, can you hear me?"

I raised my voice over the road noise. "Yep, just talk a little louder."

"You need a new truck. I don't know how you survive without Bluetooth, but that's not why I called. Can you meet me for dinner? Got an interesting story brewing."

I grinned at the familiar lecture. No way was I dumping my daddy's old truck; I'd drive it until the wheels fell off or parts became extinct. I glanced at my phone. "Sure, what time and where?"

"Mario's around seven? Where are you now?"

It was close to six and would take me another twenty minutes to reach Gray's Island. I turned onto a frontage road that ran along the marsh. "I was going out to talk to some people at Ed's yacht club but it can wait. What story are you working on?"

"Remember the bridge accident just before Hurricane Isabella?"

I snorted. "Uh yeah...since it trapped me on Belle Isle with a killer—geez, cut the high-beams!" I raised my hand to shield my eyes as a large SUV came out of nowhere to hug my back bumper. "Sorry Jess, some jerk doesn't know how to drive. He's blinding me with his lights. Hold on, I'm going to pull over since he's in such a—what the hell?"

I screeched as my truck lurched. Before I could swerve out of the path, the vehicle behind me slammed into my rear bumper again.

"Holly? What's going on? What was that noise?"

Again the SUV rammed my bumper. Fighting to keep the truck on the road, I yelled in the direction of my phone. "Someone is trying to run me off the road!" I downshifted and stomped on the gas pedal. "Colonel, sit down!"

My buddy was whining and shifting in his seat as I continued the fight to keep my truck in the middle of the narrow dirt road. I ran through the gears and flew down the back road but my attacker kept pace and the old Scout was no match.

"Jess, call 911! I'm on Old Hemsley Ridge Road. Just passed the Primitive Baptist Churc—oh my God!" Metal crumpled as the SUV slammed into me again. I fought the wheel, but momentum carried me toward the marsh.

I shouted and held my arm out to keep The Colonel in his seat as my Scout careened through the swampy grassland and hit a tree. The impact threw The Colonel to the floor and my forehead connected with the steering wheel.

My ears were ringing and there were two of everything but I managed to sit up and release my seat belt. Jessica was yelling at me through the phone but it sounded a long way off and I couldn't summon the effort to speak. Headlights illuminated the truck interior for a second before my truck was struck again, this time from the passenger side.

I held my breath as the Scout wobbled but remained upright. Blood was dripping into my eyes and the world was spinning like I'd been on a three-day bender. My attacker backed up and

I was bracing for another crash when the sweet sound of sirens pierced the air.

The last thing I heard before blacking out was the loud exhaust as my attacker sped away.

Chapter Seventeen

Every bone in my body ached. I groaned and considered if it was worth the effort of opening my eyes. Back when I was a deputy I'd been in a wreck that ended with my cruiser upside down. I'd walked away with a couple of bumps and bruises and a need for Tylenol, but this? Man, there weren't enough narcotics.

I am getting old.

"Everyone does," an amused voice I thought was Tate commented.

"Didn't mean to say that out loud." I muttered. It came out jumbled and only semi-coherent since I was doing my best not to move a muscle, not even my lips.

"Well, you did, so the jig is up. I know you're awake. Open your eyes."

"Can't, hurts too much."

Tate chuckled and I felt a prick in my arm. "That should knock out the worst of it. Give it a few seconds and you'll feel better."

I was skeptical if I'd ever feel normal again but true to his word, whatever had been in the shot worked its magic. I opened my eyes then put my hand up as a shield from the harsh overhead light.

"Bright! You're killin' me..."

Tate laughed and called me a baby but did cut the light off, leaving only a soft glow from my bedside lamp. Bedside...

"Uh, how did I get here?"

"You really were out of it!" He moved closer and grabbed my shoulders. "Here, let me help you to sit up."

Much groaning and moaning commenced until my back was resting against a mound of pillows. I muttered my thanks then stiffened. "Where's The Colonel?" Panic started to build. "Is he all right? Tate, where is he?"

"Calm down, he's fine." Tate perched on the edge of the bed and took my pulse. "Jessica took him to the vet and they are checking him over. She called a minute ago to say he's banged and bruised but none the worse for wear. She should be back in a few minutes. It's you that took the brunt of it."

Relief flooded through me and I collapsed onto the pillows. "Thank God, when we hit the tree he was thrown onto the floor and I couldn't reach him...I need to get him a car seat."

Tate snorted. "Probably, though I hope you aren't planning a repeat performance of tonight's activities."

I snorted. "No plans, trust me." I shifted on the bed and winced as my muscles protested. "What happened to my truck?"

Tate's eyes rolled heavenwards. "Really? You're worried about the truck? How about telling me what happened to you."

"Truck first." Every breath was an effort. I frowned and tentatively probed my side. "Did I break a rib?"

"You're impossible. No, your ribs are just bruised. Kind of expected when you get T-boned. You'll be fine after a couple of day's rest. Now, what happened. All Jessica said was you ran off the road."

ESCROW AND ARROWS

"Um, more like I was run off the road."

"What? Are you telling me someone deliberately ran you into the marsh?" When I nodded, Tate threw his hands up and started pacing. "That's it, this investigation is over! I knew something like this was going to happen if you kept poking into police matters, I should never have asked you to—"

"Tate!" He spun around. "Just stop, okay? I don't think this had anything to do with finding Ed's killer."

My statement took the wind out of his sails. He sank onto the edge of the bed and stared at me, a bewildered look in his eyes.

"I don't...if not the issue with Dad then what..." He frowned and shook his head. "Was it a drunk driver?"

I nibbled on my bottom lip and considered how to answer. I was saved from lying when Jessica walked in with The Colonel.

"Hey, looks who's awake!" She crossed to the bed, bringing The Colonel with her. "This very good boy needs to see you." Jess heaved my porky boy onto the bed.

Several minutes passed as my bulldog licked and snuffled me. Once assured all was well, he sighed and plastered himself to my side.

"Thanks for taking care of him, Jess. The vet said he's okay?"

"Yep, he's a little banged up, though how they can tell if a dog is bruised is beyond me. But Dr. Bailey X-rayed him and said nothing is broken." She looked at The Colonel and grinned. "He seems to think the layer of pudge cushioned him."

Tate snorted and I glared at him. "Stop it, he's just a little plump." The quietness of the house finally hit me and I frowned. "Hey, where's Mama?" There was no way my mother was home and not hovering over me.

Tate shrugged. "No one was here when I brought you home, don't you remember?"

My memory of what happened after the cops arrived was hazy at best. "Um, I vaguely recall the police arriving and then the EMTs." I looked up at him. "How did you know?"

"Jessica called me and I met the ambulance at the ER." He came closer and leaned in to stare into my eyes. "You aren't technically concussed, but you must have hit your head pretty hard if you can't remember refusing to remain in the hospital."

Ah, it was coming back to me now. I drifted in and out during transport to the hospital and only woke up when someone stuck a needle into my arm. "Yeah, it's a wonder I didn't dent the steering wheel. Speaking of, where is my truck?"

154

Tate rolled his eyes but Jessica grinned and provided me with an answer. "Told you she'd be worried about The Colonel and the truck, in that order. Should have bet you a hundred bucks, Tate."

I laughed, or started to, but the action sent pain through my rib cage. "No more jokes, y'all!" I looked at Jessica. "Give it to me straight. Is Daddy's truck toast?"

She grimaced. "Eh, I'm no expert but it looked pretty bad. I arrived on scene just as you were being loaded into the ambulance. Since Tate was heading to the hospital, I stuck around and waited on the tow truck then took The Colonel to Doctor Bailey. I had them tow it to Fred's garage, is that okay?"

I blew out a breath I hadn't realized I was holding. "Thank you, that's perfect. If anyone can save the Scout, it's Fred." I looked over at Tate. "Mama must still be at her garden club meeting. Ms. Lou Lou was hosting tonight and I dropped her off. I hate to ask, but can you run over and pick Mama up?"

Tate got to his feet. "Of course, you gonna be all right while I'm gone?"

I summoned a reassuring smile I was far from feeling. "Sure, I'm just a little sore and Jessica is here. We'll be fine."

"If you're sure…" He glanced between Jess and me for a second then shrugged and left, but I could tell by the look on his face he knew something was up as did Jessica. As soon as we saw the lights of Tate's car fade, she pounced.

"Okay, what's going on?"

I didn't bother prevaricating. Not for nothing had my friend won investigative journalist awards. "I was threatened today."

Her eyes widened. "What? By whom? Was it to do with your murder investigation?"

I drew a deep breath and exhaled harshly. "The who is J.T. Minton and the why…" I shrugged. "I don't know for sure."

"Whoa, Minton threatened you? That makes no sense." Her brows drew together. "Maybe you misinterpreted. What exactly did he say?"

I didn't take offense at her skepticism. As far as I knew, I was the only person that felt something was off about Minton. Everyone else in Sanctuary Bay treated him like a founding father. "After I asked him where he was at the time of Ed's murder, he basically said that he was surprised someone that had had a brush with death wasn't treading more carefully."

Her mouth dropped open. "Wow, no misinterpreting that!"

"No, his meaning was crystal clear."

We sat in silence for a few minutes, each ruminating on the turn of events that had left me battered and bruised. Finally, Jessica huffed and shook her head.

"Are you thinking J.T. ran you off the road?"

Was I? Until I'd told her about the barely veiled threat, I hadn't connected the two incidents. Now that she'd linked the two... "For all that I don't like or trust the man, I can't see him doing something so blatant. At least, not personally. He's more than capable of hiring someone though."

Her brows shot up. "Wow, you really don't like the man!"

I shrugged. "It's not that, really. He's just shady somehow. I can't define it, but he sets off all of my internal alarm bells."

She shook her head. "Well, I've learned to trust your instincts, but if he did instigate your wreck, does that mean he killed Ed?"

"That's just it. He has an alibi, and based on the way he reacted when Mama told him Royal Ventures has discovered irregularities in the marina project's escrow account, he was visibly shaken. I'd dismissed him as a suspect."

"Wait, there's money missing?"

I nodded. "Yeah, I was gonna tell you over dinner. Mama and I talked to Stephanie Gilroy before we went to see Minton, and she told me that Ed owes her a lot of money. She tried to collect and found his office in an uproar. The escrow account is empty."

"My word, this just gets more and more complicated. You think Ed stole the money?"

"I do, though I don't think the killer found it." I told her about the state of Ava's house and how Mama hadn't noticed any signs of a search when she was trespassing on Ed's yacht.

"Well then, where's the money?"

"No idea but I have to wonder if Ava has it."

She blinked. "What? You think she staged her condo to look like something happened to her and then ran off with the money?"

"Don't know, but it's certainly possible."

We lapsed into silence again until Jess cleared her throat.

"So what are you going to do now?"

I sighed. "The two suspects I had are in the clear. Ava might have done it, but if she did, it'll be up to the police to find her. When you called I was on my way to Gray's Island. For lack of better ideas, I'll go out tomorrow and talk to the dockmaster and the security guards."

Jess frowned. "What do you hope to find?"

"Well, because of the time Ed was killed, it had to be someone with access to the marina. That means a boat owner with an access code to the gate or someone living in the condos."

She nodded. "Makes sense, but how many people are you talking about? Sounds like a lot of people to interview."

"Not really. The marina has only been open a few weeks. I saw two skiffs along with Ed's yacht, so that's two boat owners to check out. Six condos are completed: John McGrath lives in one, Ava has one, leaving me with at most four people with access and I can't say for sure all of those finished condos are inhabited. Might be fewer people."

"That's more manageable. So you've decided the motive was the missing money and lack of progress on the development?"

"Eh...it's my working theory, but I haven't ruled out a spurned lover or an angry environmental activist."

"Sounds like you have a solid plan. Do you need my help?"

I bit my lip and considered her offer. Things would go more quickly if I let her do some of the legwork, but she'd mentioned a developing story and I hated to impose. "Maybe? Let me talk to the dockmaster first. I might get everything I need. I appreciate the offer though. I know how busy you are. You mentioned working on a story involving the bridge accident. What's that about?"

Jessica smiled. "Oh girl, you are not gonna believe what I've uncovered!" She settled cross legged on the end of my bed. "So, you know how the county dump truck wrecked and damaged the swing bridge."

I snorted. "Uh, yeah...ended up stuck at Pennington Place with a killer. I also know you were investigating that accident and I seem to recall something about an insurance adjuster?"

Jess grinned. "Bingo! The adjuster found some things amiss with the maintenance records and started digging. Guess what he found?"

"No idea, spill!"

"Would you be shocked to learn that the dump truck in question was over ten years old?"

I frowned. "No? Why is that significant? Was it not maintained properly?"

She smirked. "The accident was caused by a broken hydraulic something or other which is what set the auditor to snooping. Seems those things don't go bad on new trucks."

"Wait, you said the truck was old..."

"It is, but not according to the public works department's records. Those show that the whole fleet was replaced with new vehicles sixteen months ago."

"But that means…"

She laughed. "Yep, someone has been fiddling the books so to speak. I've pulled FOIA requests for the budget, the requisition and purchasing forms, and the maintenance logs. The really interesting thing about that wrecked truck is the VIN number. It matches the registration which says the truck is new."

I tipped my head back against the pillows and considered what Jessica had said. At least one dump truck did not match county records. The odds were good that the rest of the fleet was also not as advertised.

Changing VIN numbers made me think of car thieves running a chop shop. Considering the truck belonged to the county, there was only one way fraud at that level could be pulled off. "Jess, in order to pass that old truck off as a new vehicle…"

Her smile was smug. "Yep, someone in that purchasing department has to be involved and that leads to?"

I gulped. "Preston Spruill."

Chapter Eighteen

The first thing I did the next morning was head to Fred's garage. Unfortunately, Mama insisted on accompanying me and badgered me the entire ride out to the county.

"You should be in bed. That was a serious accident, young lady, and your body needs rest."

"Yes ma'am." That had been my standard reply for what felt like hours, but no matter how many times I uttered it, Mama continued to hassle me.

"...and why you insist upon going to Fred's is beyond me." She huffed. "That truck is almost as old as you are! High time it was put out to pasture. Why don't you visit Buck's and get a new one? And another thing. Since you insist on going against doctor's orders, wouldn't our time be better spent looking for Ed's killer?"

Drawing a deep breath and counting to ten, I explained, "Mama, I'm not interested in another truck, new or not." I flipped on my signal and turned into Fred's garage. "And I am going to visit Gray's Island Marina just as soon as I finish here. Sit tight, I'll only be a minute."

Mama started yammering a rebuttal but I slammed the car door. My nerves were hanging by a thread and I wasn't confident I'd be able to keep a civil tongue in my head if she continued to fuss.

Fred's shop was situated on acres of land out in the middle of nowhere. A concrete building sat near the front of the property, surrounded by vehicles in various states of repair, while the rear portion held an auto graveyard. Visiting was like coming home.

There were several competent mechanics in Noble County, but my father had always patronized Fred's and over the years, they'd become friends and fishing buddies. I always felt closer to my dad when I visited the garage, but today was bittersweet. I'd told Mama I didn't want a new truck, but I feared not having a choice. The Scout was old and no longer manufactured. Depending on the damage, it might be impossible to repair.

"Holly Daye, as I live and breathe." Fred came around the desk and enveloped me in a bear hug. "Child, what on earth did you do to your daddy's truck?"

I returned the hug, closing my eyes as I breathed in the mingled odors of cigarette smoke and motor oil. Tears welled and I realized I was not nearly as okay as I'd let on to Tate and Mama.

Sniffing, I pulled away from Fred and looked through the glass door that led to the shop. My Scout was in the farthest bay with her hood raised, though the body was blocked by two other cars.

"How bad is she, Fred?"

His gaze roamed over me for a second and he clucked his tongue. "You look like ya been rode hard and put away wet." He cocked his head toward the garage door. "C'mon, let's take a look."

I trailed behind him, my stomach in knots. How bad was it? Was this the end? Would I have to part with the last piece of my father? We walked into the bay and I gasped. My poor truck!

"Now, now, it looks worse than it is! Don't give up on her yet! Ol' Fred will have her right as rain in no time."

Chest tight, I walked around the Scout, assessing the damage. The rear bumper was shoved into the tailgate so far I couldn't tell where one started and the other ended. The spare tire was gone, and the passenger side door was a crumpled mess.

The front bumper had helped control the damage when I crashed into the tree, but the grill was toast, and I wondered how Fred had managed to pop the hood. A sour taste filled my mouth as I realized how lucky I was to be walking upright. Had I been in Mama's car, or even a newer truck, I wouldn't have gotten off so lightly.

"Uh, you really think," my voice cracked. I cleared my throat, swallowed hard, and tried again. "Looks bad, Fred. Is it really repairable?"

He patted my shoulder. "O'course it is! You just have some faith in old Fred. Gonna take a while cuz parts ain't growin' on trees, but she'll be good as new, promise." He looked at the Scout and whistled. "Yer lucky to be standin' here, child. Good thing ya were drivin' somethin' made o' good ol' American steel."

"Was just thinkin' that. They don't make them like this anymore."

He snorted. "Sure don't." He stared at me through narrowed eyes. "Mind tellin' me who ya tangled with to wind up in this mess?"

Blinking in surprise, I stammered, "I uh, don't know what you mean. It was an accident—"

"Please." He snorted. "Weren't no accident did this kind of damage. Looks ta me like someone tried to run ya off the road."

I started to deny it, but Fred was sharp and I knew it'd be useless. I sighed and nodded. "They did but I don't know who or why."

Proving he was smart as a fox; Fred folded his arms across his burly chest and looked down his nose. "Might be on account of ya always stickin' yer nose into police business."

He was semi-right, though I had no intention of admitting it. I forced a laugh. "Nah, more likely some drunk teen with road rage." I tipped my head toward the parking lot. "Mama's waiting so I've got to run. You let me know when I need to pay ya, okay?"

He nodded, though the look he gave me said he knew I was full of manure. "Will do. Expectin' a new door next week and the radiator will be fixed by the end of the day. I'll start you a tab. Know yer good for it."

Hoping I wasn't going to end up draining my savings account or needing to sell my first born, I waved goodbye and headed to the car. Being run off the road had put me on alert. It also forced me to accept the fact that I needed to put my gun in the glove box. I hadn't carried, much less fired my weapon since I'd been shot. But, Mama often rode with me and should something happen again ...

I tried to find a compelling reason for Mama to go home without telling her the truth. The reality was, someone in the county had painted a bullseye on me.

The bell over the door jingled as Mama and I entered the dockmaster's office. I'd been unable to convince her she had more important things to do, but I had stressed she was to let me do the talking. It remained to be seen if she'd listen.

"Mornin'. Dockmaster in?"

A younger man seated in front of several computer monitors looked up for a second and pointed toward the docks. "Bobby's checkin' on a boat that slipped its mooring. Be back in minute. Somethin' I can help you with?"

I'd known Bobby Raymond since high school and from what I remembered, he'd always been a law-and-order kind of guy. I'd anticipated a struggle before he'd part with the information I was seeking, so I jumped on the opportunity to coax it from someone else.

Dawning a bright smile, I nodded. "Sure hope so. I'm thinking of moving my boat from the city marina. How many slips do you have available?"

The kid, Chip according to his nametag, pulled down a log book and flipped it open. "The marina has three docks designated for day use and currently fifteen slips are ready. When construction is completed, there will be seventy."

"Oh good, and how much is it to dock my skiff here?"

"Four fifty a month and that includes wi-fi, trash service, water, and electric hook-up." He started tapping keys on a laptop. "What's your membership number?"

"Membership?"

Chip looked up. "Yes, for the yacht club. Only members or residents of Pine Harbor can rent the long-term slips."

I donned a sad expression. "Oh, I was under the impression anyone could rent them." I stood on tiptoe and peered out the picture window that faced the docks. "Perhaps the yacht club would make an exception. All money spends the same and it doesn't look like they are doing much business..." Aside from Ed's yacht, there were only two skiffs in the marina.

Chip grinned. "Yes, it does, but I doubt they'll ignore the rules." He tipped his head toward the docks. "We currently only have those three, but there's a membership drive right now, and once the rest of the homes are built in Pine Harbor, we'll fill up."

"I see. Well, that's disappointing but maybe I'll join the club. Thanks for your help!"

I snapped The Colonel's leash to get him moving and ushered Mama outside. We'd barely taken five steps when she started in on me.

"What was that all about? You should have asked him if he was here during the ball or did he see anyone on the docks that night! We have nothing to prove Dean didn't kill Ed and we need to—"

"I got all I needed from him, Mama. Now I want to see who's living in the condos and how many are women." I started walking toward the guard shack that stood at the entrance to Pine Harbor. "You coming?"

Mama continued to pester me. "We know John McGrath and Ava have condos. There're only four more finished, right?" I nodded and tried to keep her moving. "We could find out who bought them from Stephanie. I don't see why we need to talk to this guard, and why does it matter if any of them are women?"

"Because, one of the motives we listed is an angry lover and I don't think Ed played for both teams. Yes, I could ask Stephanie who she sold them to, but she wouldn't know who was at home the night of the ball."

My response shut Mama up and soon we reached the guard booth. I gave her the let-me-do-the-talking look and knocked on the window.

The guard slid the window open and smiled. "Help you with something, miss?"

"Hi, Mama and I were just looking around while we wait for our realtor." I glanced at my watch and sighed. "She should have been here twenty minutes ago. Can't imagine what's keeping her..."

"You waitin' on Ms. Gilroy to show you the place?" I nodded and he shook his head. "Well, doubt she'll be here any time soon.

Everything is in a bit of an uproar. Y'all didn't hear about the murder?"

I was about to reply when Mama came closer and pressed her hand to her chest. "Gracious, there was a murder here?"

He tipped his head in greeting to Mama. "Yes ma'am. Fella that owned the place, but don't you worry none, I don't think there's a psycho runnin' 'round the place. Ol' Ed probably had lots of enemies."

I frowned. "What makes you say that?" I offered my hand. "I'm Holly, by the way, and this is my mother, Effie."

"Pleased to meet ya ladies. I'm Henry, and I say that because I been dealing with protestors for weeks. Lots of people don't want this place built. But don't let that stop ya from buying in Pine Harbor. It's a real nice place. Got tennis courts, indoor and outdoor pools; they tell me there's gonna be a golf course, too!"

Mama shook her head. "I don't know. Even with all of that, it's not much security if someone has been murdered. No offense to you, I'm sure you do a good job, but I'm an old woman living alone."

Henry frowned. "I uh, don't know what to say other than what I told ya. Really we ain't had nothing go wrong until this thing with Mr. Ed, even the protestors have been polite. Ask anybody, they'll tell ya!"

"Hmmm, you know that might not be a bad idea, Henry. I think I'll do that. If you'll let us in, I'll see if anyone is home." I hid a smile as Mama led the guard right where we wanted him.

Henry winced. "Eh, I'm not supposed to do that, Ms. Effie, but I'd make an exception for ya, only I don't think any of our residents are home. There're only the six of them right now." He worried at his lower lip and stared off into the distance for a second. "Mr. and Mrs. Johnson have the first unit as you come off out of the marina, but they been on a cruise since last Monday and won't return until Sunday."

"Is there anyone else living here?"

Henry nodded. "Yes ma'am, Mr. Born lives next door to the Johnsons. He's an artist and has a gallery over in Sanctuary Bay...hey, ya might find Mr. McGrath at the club, he's the chairman ya know."

Mama nodded. "I've known Johnny for years; I might just do that." She turned and acted as if she were going to the yacht club then turned back and shook her head. "On second thought, I'd rather speak with a woman, single preferably. A man won't have the same concerns, you understand." She smiled sweetly. "Are there any single women living here?"

Henry's brow furrowed and he scratched his head. "Well now, there's Miss Ava, but she's uh...well she's out of town I think and uh..." I tried not to laugh as Henry tied himself up in knots to avoid telling us of another suspected crime on the grounds. I decided to help him out.

"Ava Walker?" I pretended ignorance, curious to see what he'd say. "The interior designer?" Looking relieved, Henry nodded. "I didn't realize she lived here."

"Yes ma'am. Only like I said, she's not here right now." He squirmed and looked to the ground. "You ah, could talk to , Ms. Osbourne. She works at the Sea Islands Bank. She isn't a resident but I see her around a lot, especially talking with Mr. Whitten. Pretty sure she works with him or somethin'."

I frowned. Another person to speak to. "Thanks, Henry, I'll do that!"

Beside me, Mama drew a harsh breath. I frowned at her but she just shook her head and mouthed, *later*. "Thank you Henry, we have to go into town so we'll do that. You said Osbourne?"

"Yep, Serena's her name and I think she does something in one of the offices. Leastways I know she ain't a teller."

We thanked him again and headed back to the car. I loaded The Colonel into the back seat and then waited for Mama to get her seat belt on. I started the car and turned on the heat before turning in my seat. "Okay, what was all that about? You looked funny when Henry mentioned Serena Osbourne. That's the woman you said had loose morals, right?"

Mama smirked. "Oh yes, but that isn't all I know about her. Head into town and I'll tell you what I learned about our banker lady at the garden club meeting last night."

Chapter Nineteen

D ean's attorney had arranged for Mama to visit. I pulled into the parking lot of the county jail and then swiveled to face her.

"So let me get this straight. Serena Osbourne was the woman who had a fling with Ed the year I was recovering from the shooting."

"Yes, she's the one I told you I couldn't remember the details about. But Lou Lou was more than happy to fill me in! It seems that Serena had an affair with Ed while he was still married. Ed's wife found out and that was what led to his third divorce."

"Okay, so she's as bad as you said, but since we don't bank there, I can't see where her morals or lack of them are a big deal."

"Hold on, Holly Marie, this has nothing to do with having money in that bank!" She sighed and shook her head. "My goodness, you're missing the point. She broke up Ed's marriage but that wasn't all. They continued their affair, and once Ed's divorce was finalized she started spreading it all over town that they were engaged. Then he dumped her."

It was all gossip to me and even after Mama explained I had to confess to not seeing how it was relevant to Ed's murder. Mama huffed.

"Not see...Holly, you said Ed might have been killed by a jilted lover and you can't get much more jilted than Serena!"

She had a point, small though I thought it might be. "It's possible I suppose, but that was years ago. Why kill him now?"

Mama huffed again and rolled her eyes. "How should I know? But you be sure and ask her where she was that night. Now I'm off to see Dean." She sighed. "Poor man, I wish that judge would listen to reason and at least grant him bail!"

My eyes widened as I recalled my plan to get character references for Dean. Crud, with everything that had happened, it had slipped my mind. I added visiting his former nurse to my list right after I talked to Serena Osbourne.

"Oh, there's Paul Matthews waiting by the door. I'll talk to you later, dear."

She started to exit the vehicle when she turned and asked, "Do you think Serena was in on it with Ed?"

Did I? I shrugged. "Only one way to find out. You go see Dean. I'll stop by for a chat with the banker."

Mama clucked her tongue. "Oh dear, I'd hoped we were close to solving this thing so poor Dean can come home. Now what are we going to do? If she didn't murder Ed then who did?"

Tears were welling in my mother's eyes and guilt slammed into me. She was hurting and I could do nothing to mitigate it. Searching for something to encourage her, I relented and told her my plan. "We'll figure out who killed Ed, Mama, don't worry. And I might have a way to get Dean released on bail. You go visit with him and I'll see what I can do, okay?"

She started to press for details but the attorney was waiting to escort her into the jail. "Don't mention anything to Dean, Mama. The visiting areas are monitored and I don't want Detective Brannon to know what we're up to. Have a nice time and I'll pick you up in an hour."

One hour before I had to pick Mama up. Just enough time to knock two more things off my list.

The commercial loan department was in a similar state of chaos as what Stephanie had described happening at Royal Ventures. After sitting in the lobby for ten minutes with no one coming to assist me, The Colonel and I set off to snoop.

People were walking in and out of cubicles carrying piles of folders and talking in hushed but panicked voices while others were manning the phones. No one stopped me, so I walked past and ventured down a hallway lined with offices.

Reading the names on the doors, I stopped at Serena Osbourne's. It was partially cracked so I nudged it open wider and stuck my head in.

"Can I help you?"

Serena was a pretty woman probably a few years younger than me. Her glossy dark hair was pulled into an elegant twist at the nape of her neck, Diamonds sparkled at her earlobes and a delicate charm bracelet dangled from her wrist.

She was dressed conservatively, but even my lack of fashion sense recognized a high-end suit. From head to toe she screamed money and power.

Surrounded by a mess of boxes and files, she also exuded a lot of hostility.

Figuring she would appreciate directness, I got straight to the point. "Hi, I'm Holly Daye and—"

"I know who you are."

Great. Once again, my reputation preceded me. If the paper didn't stop reporting that I helped solve crimes in Sanctuary Bay, I was gonna be run out of town on a rail or at least be uninvited to the community pig pickin'.

Choosing to ignore the implications in her statement, I smiled and invited myself farther into her office. The top of her desk was nearly bare; only a lamp, phone, and a stack of papers remained. Everything else appeared to be in the boxes at her feet. Another quick glance and my eye caught a glimpse of blue among the papers. A very familiar dark blue used by the passport office.

Combined with the boxes, I made an educated guess and asked, "Going somewhere?"

Serena scowled. "As it happens, yes, though not the trip I'd planned." She tossed the last stack of papers into a box and dropped into her chair. "Before you ask, I've been fired, Ms. Daye."

My brows rose. "Oh, I'm sorry. Does it have anything to do with the money missing from the Pine Harbor escrow account?"

Her expression turned stony, except for her eyes. They were glaring daggers. "You *are* well informed. Guess that's how you keep solving all of these crimes." She snorted. "But, to answer your question, I was fired because that rat Ed Whitten embezzled the escrow funds."

"About that. I'm given to understand you were his account manager. How could he have done that without your knowing?"

Her lip curled. "And that is the question of the hour. Get in line, the auditors are ahead of you."

Ah, that explained the commotion in the outer offices. "He didn't leave a trail?"

She shook her head. "Not that it's any of your business, but no, I don't know how he did it. Frankly, it's no longer my problem." She rose. "Now, if that's all? I have packing to do."

"Um, just a few more questions if you don't mind." Her expression said she very much did, but I ignored it. "I've heard you and Ed were a couple a while back. You didn't think handling his account was a conflict of interest?"

Her eyes narrowed for a second and then she laughed. "The only conflict between Ed and me was over the condo I paid for and he didn't build. I'm a victim too, Ms. Daye."

"You invested in Pine Harbor?"

She smiled but the action held no humor. "Some business woman I am, right? Should have known not to trust him with my money."

For all of his faults, Ed Whitten and Royal Ventures had earned a solid reputation in the county. To my knowledge, there'd never been a hint of impropriety in his business dealings—before now anyway. Unless Serena's comment was based on something other than business.

The gossip about Ed and his many affairs popped into my head and I asked, "Why? Because you already knew he couldn't be trusted with your heart?"

A dull flush stained her cheeks, but to her credit, she hid her anger behind a mocking smile. "You *have* been busy. For the record? My affair with Ed was just a fun-filled fling. We both knew it wasn't serious."

I recalled the gossip that suggested otherwise.

"So you didn't expect him to marry you."

Serena laughed, a deep full-throated roar. When she calmed down, she wiped her eyes and smiled. "Thanks, I needed that. And no, any woman in a relationship with Ed knows the score, whether she accepts it or not is on her. After three failed marriages and a mountain of alimony payments, he was never going to tie that knot again."

She chuckled again and walked over to a closet. Pulling on a beautiful red coat, she picked up the box she'd been filling and headed for the door. "You want to talk; you'll have to follow me. I'm done here."

I trotted along beside her as she made her way to the employee parking lot. "So you and Ed had a good working relationship, despite the breakup?"

Serena stopped walking and looked at me. "I told you; it was nothing, not much more than a one-night stand."

She continued toward her car and I pulled out my heavy ammo. "So then why were you seen having an intense conversation with him outside of the restrooms during the Valentine's Day ball?"

She snorted and hit the fob to unlock her car. "Wouldn't have pegged you as someone that indulges in idle gossip."

"I'm not, but this doesn't fit that bill. What were the two of you discussing, because my source said you jumped back and looked guilty when they interrupted."

A look of annoyance marred her features for a second and then she laughed and opened the trunk to deposit the box she carried. "It's none of your business, but if it'll get you out of my hair, we were discussing my unfinished condo. He promised it would be ready in three weeks. Satisfied?"

"I see." But I didn't believe her. Mama had said they'd had their heads together and were whispering. That wasn't necessary for something so mundane. But I'd play along. "So you aren't living at Pine Harbor?"

"No, hence the word unfinished. It's mostly complete but I'm not living with plywood floors and unpainted walls." She slammed the trunk closed and nudged me aside so she could get to the driver's side door. "Now, if you'll excuse me? I have to get on with my life."

I put my hand on the car door to stop her from opening it. "Just for kicks, where were you between 1:00 a.m. and 3:00 a.m the night after the ball?"

Serena snorted and rolled her eyes. "Home, of course. Same place I'm going now."

"One more thing." I ignored the annoyed look and even allowed her access to her car. I could be polite when it suited me. "Are you a member of the yacht club or just a resident of Pine Harbor?"

"Since I don't own a boat, much less a yacht, what would be the point?" She pulled the door from my hand. "Run along, Ms. Daye, I'm not the killer."

That remained to be seen, but she'd said nothing to indicate a deeper look into her life was necessary. Unless something surfaced to change that, I had bigger fish to fry.

I headed across town to the home of Doris Reed, Doctor Sawyer's longtime nurse. Hopefully she'd tell me something that would help because I was fresh out of ideas.

Doris was a tiny woman that reminded me of a bird. Not only was she small in stature, but she flittered around the fussily decorated living room like a hummingbird bouncing from flower to flower hunting nectar.

I accepted the offer of tea in hopes she'd finally sit down; she was making The Colonel nervous, and me too, if I were honest.

The clink of china heralded her return. "Here we are..." She set an overly laden silver tray on the coffee table and poured me a cup. "Sugar? Milk? Lemon?"

"Just sugar, please." I accepted the delicate cup and saucer and prayed I didn't spill or break it. Surrounded by so many dainty things, I felt like the proverbial bull in the china shop, and with an actual bulldog in the mix, I feared Ms. Doris's room wasn't going to survive our visit unscathed.

She poured herself a cup and then offered me a plate filled with tiny cakes and sandwiches. How had she prepared all of it in the minutes I was waiting, or did she indulge in that manner regardless of visitors?

My questions were destined to remain unanswered because Doris had been on a trip down memory lane since I'd mentioned the reason for my visit.

I sipped my tea and let my mind wander as she continued extolling the doctor's virtues.

"Yes indeed, Doctor Dean is a lovely man. I'm heartbroken over what's happened. Why anyone would believe him capable of such a ghastly thing...ridiculous. Why, in forty years I never saw him lose his temper, well except for one time but that was completely justified!"

Not really interested but ready to move the needle on her broken record, I asked, "What was justified, Ms. Doris?"

"Hmm? Oh, it was just a little squabble with..." Her hand shook and tea sloshed over the edge of the cup. "Oh how clumsy of me, let me just..." She set the cup and saucer down and reached for a napkin, her hand still trembling slightly. Her gaze bounced around, gliding across the room and then the coffee table. Anywhere but toward me.

"Goodness I've forgotten the jam! You simply must try one of my scones with the freezer jam I got from Inez Benson. She makes it from strawberries she grows herself." She leaped up and scurried to the kitchen, calling out that she'd be back in a jiffy.

Now that was interesting. The little old lady had been calm, well as calm as I think she ever managed, and chatting away then as soon as I asked about Dean losing his temper she got flustered and ran off. Curiosity might have killed the cat, but I was keen to know what she was referring to. Besides, I was more of a dog person anyway.

Doris settled across from me and offered a plate of fluffy scones. I wasn't hungry but The Colonel was eyeing the plate, and I needed to keep her happy so I broke the pastry open and slathered it with jam as I gently guided her back to the conversation.

"This looks wonderful, Ms. Doris, and I think my dog wants to try if you don't mind. He's such a glutton, I'm sure he won't leave a crumb."

"Be my guest, dear. He's such a handsome boy, I'm sure he has impeccable manners. You know Doctor Dean used to have a little Jack Russell and he'd bring him into the office sometimes. The patients seemed more at ease when Prancer was there." She sighed and sat back in chair. "Everything was so much easier back then. I don't know what the world is coming to; I really don't. It isn't at all surprising someone committed murder because everyone seems to be so angry nowadays. Why I was shopping the other day and a woman got into an argument with the poor cashier...gracious, but the language she used. That wouldn't have happened in my day, people knew how to control their tempers."

I hid a smile as she gave me an opening to redirect the conversation. "Yes ma'am, I agree, we are certainly seeing less civilized behavior than how I was raised. But speaking of tempers, you mentioned Doctor Sawyer losing his?"

For a minute I thought she'd change the subject, but after fidgeting with her napkin and then adding milk to her tea, she sighed and clucked her tongue. "I shouldn't have mentioned it and really, it has no bearing on this dreadful situation—"

"Please, Ms. Doris, I'd like to hear about it."

She glanced at me and then looked down at the floor. "Well, if you insist, but you have to understand it was all in defense of his patient. Doctor Sawyer would never have stooped to such a level if not provoked and—"

"Yes ma'am, I understand but what happened?"

Doris bit her lower lip then drew a deep breath and nodded. "It was just a few months before he retired. We were still seeing a few patients but most had transferred to that new practice next to the hospital. Anyway, Doctor Dean had been treating a woman for depression. Poor thing, he tried and tried to get her to see a therapist but she refused. So you see he had no choice, and then oh, it was so dreadful…"

Through fits and starts and a minor burst of crying, I managed to pry the story from her. And what a mess. I'd visited with the intention of helping Dean only to leave with the uncomfortable feeling I'd been hunting for Ed's killer in the wrong place all along.

Chapter Twenty

The rest of the day went by in a blur. I picked Mama up from visiting Dean, ran some errands, and checked in at Glitter and Garlands on autopilot. Talking with Doris had left my mind spinning in circles and I had no idea what to do with the information I'd gleaned.

Mama had cooked supper so I volunteered for dish duty thinking I'd be left in peace. Unfortunately, she picked up a towel and started drying, chatting all the while.

"...and I told Dean that you are close to finding the real killer. He asked me to express his gratitude which of course I assured him I would and—"

"Mama..." I paused in the act of scrubbing a skillet. "Why did you tell him that?"

She huffed. "Why? Because it's the truth! Surely you have some idea...what's the matter? You've gone very pale. Are you feeling poorly? I knew you should have been resting after the accident!" She grabbed my arm and started to pull me toward the stairs. "Now you go right up to bed and I'll bring you—"

"Stop!" I shook loose of her grip and returned to the sink. "I'm fine, totally fine, and I wish you'd stop harping about my health. I also wish you hadn't told Dean he's about to be set free! You shouldn't have gotten his hopes up."

She frowned and started to reply when someone knocked on the door. "Now, who could that be..." She went to the back door. "Why it's Tate! Tate is here, Holly Marie. Come inside, it's turning chilly again and the radio said we'll have a hard frost. I do hope my hydrangeas will be okay, I never got around to covering them...here Tate, sit down and have a cup of coffee."

I met Tate's gaze and smirked. He looked a bit shell-shocked but then Mama tended to have that effect on most people. I always wondered how she talked so long without taking a breath.

"Now then, here's your coffee and would you tell that daughter of mine she needs to be resting? Just before you arrived she went white as a sheet and I tried to get her to go up to bed..." Mama sighed and shook her head. "But you know how stubborn she is."

Tate looked at me and waggled his brows. "I do indeed, Ms. Effie."

I rolled my eyes and turned to finish the dishes. "If y'all are finished assaulting my character, perhaps we can discuss something useful?"

I regretted the flippant comment as soon as the words left my mouth because Mama took that to mean talking about finding Ed's killer and with what I'd learned from Doris, I was afraid I already knew who the culprit was.

"Holly Marie? Do you think that's a possibility?"

I'd been trying to shake off my reverie and focus on Mama and Tate's conversation but I'd definitely missed something important. Stalling for time, I rinsed out the sink and dried my hands before turning to face them.

"Um...I missed part of what you were saying, Mama. Might what be a possibility?"

As expected, my mother huffed and scolded me for day dreaming before getting to the point. "...and then I asked if you thought it was Ava that killed Ed after all. We've eliminated everyone else."

My mouth went dry. This was why I'd avoided discussing the situation Dean was in. Tate and Mama were staring at me expectantly and there was nothing left to keep me from joining them at the table.

Feeling like I was walking to the gallows, I crossed the room and sat in the chair farthest from them. What I had to say was not going to go over well.

"Uh, about that." I shot an apologetic look toward Tate and told myself to suck it up and get on with it. "I had the idea character references might help get bail for Dean, so while you were visiting at the jail, I stopped by Doris Reed's."

Tate's brows rose. "Dad's old nurse? That was good thinking, Holly. Did she give you a recommendation or agree to speak to the judge?"

"Not exactly..."

Mama frowned. "What does that mean? Is she going to help Dean or not?"

"Uh, yes, she's willing to go before Judge Calder if he'll allow it, but um, she told me something that uh, makes me wonder if we should proceed with seeking bail."

Mama gasped and Tate made an exclamation of surprise, but at least I'd given voice to my concerns. Not that it made me feel better.

Mama was the first to find her voice. "Why on earth would we not try and get Dean out of jail? He's miserable. He assures me they are treating him well, but you know that can't be true and a man his age shouldn't be subjected to such a thing! We have to find out who really killed Ed and—"

"Mama, Doris told me something that makes me think the killer is already in custody."

My statement sidelined my mother. Her expression was one of confusion but Tate was not so easily befuddled.

Scowl marring his handsome features, he stared at me and quietly asked. "Are you suggesting my father is guilty?"

"What? Oh good Lord, don't be silly Tate! Whatever gave you such an idea? Holly just meant...well I'm not sure what she meant but, but certainly not that!"

I squirmed as Mama joined Tate in staring at me like I'd grown another head. "Holly Marie? Tell Tate he's being ridiculous, that you weren't suggesting—"

"I can't do that, Mama." I whispered as I met Tate's eyes and silently begged for something. Forgiveness, acceptance? I didn't know what I wanted from him, but it certainly wasn't the look of disgust he was directing at me.

His gaze never wavered. Mama fell silent and it felt like Tate and I were the only two in the room as his eyes sent me a message I had never wished to hear from him. I took it as long as I could and then dropped my gaze to the floor.

"Don't..." I choked up and had to start again. "D-don't look at me like that, Tate. I take no pleasure in—"

"Then why are you saying this?" He went from zero to sixty in an instant. Slamming his fist onto the table before jumping up to pace the floor. "How can you sit there and suggest my father, a man revered in this town for over forty years, might be guilty of murder?"

"If you'll just calm down—"

"Calm down? You expect me to sit down and discuss this like we're talking about the weather?" He stalked across the kitchen and stood at the sink, his hands clenching the counter's edge as he stared out the window. "Why? Why even suggest such a thing, Holly?"

He'd managed to rein in his anger, but there was an edge to his voice that set my heart pounding and my stomach rolling. We'd never, since the day we agreed to be more than casual friends, spoken to each other with such anger. More than that, Tate had looked at me like I'd betrayed him. It cut me to the quick.

"Tate..." I walked over and laid my hand on his shoulder. He stiffened but didn't jerk away, which I took as a hopeful sign. Not that what I had to say was going to make things better.

Deciding it was better to just rip the Band-Aid off, I returned to the table. Clearing my throat several times, I managed to find my voice.

"Mama, do you remember telling me about Ava Walker's mother?"

She frowned. "Yes, what about her? What does this have to do with Dean?"

"I'm getting to that." I glanced at Tate. He was still facing the window but he'd once again stiffened as if he knew he needed to brace for what was coming.

"It seems that Karen, that was Ava's mother's name, was a patient of Doctor Sawyer's. She um, well she had some mental health issues, and according to Doris, he tried to get her to see a therapist. She refused, so he continued to treat her as best he could."

Mama was worrying at her lower lip and giving me nervous glances as her gaze moved between me and Tate. I gave her a reassuring smile and focused on Tate as I continued.

"Doris said that Doctor Sawyer developed a deeper relationship with Karen," Mama gasped and Dean spun around to scowl at me. I held up my hand to forestall their comments. "Not like that y'all. She was in her early thirties, and Doris said Dean thought of her as a daughter, or maybe a niece? I don't know, but he was fond of her and took her problems to heart more than was usual for a patient. Doris seemed to think it had something to do with him getting ready to retire. She was one of his last patients and that was also just after your mother died, Tate."

My attempt to ease into the truth only served to anger Tate.

"Get to the point, Holly." He demanded through clenched teeth.

Okay then...I drew a deep breath and exhaled slowly. "Karen was involved with a man that, um, that worsened her depression and anxiety. At the time, Dean didn't know who it was, but he saw the effects of the relationship and urged her to end it. But Karen didn't listen."

I looked at Mama. "It was Ed Whitten. He was having an affair with Karen. This was while he was married to his second wife I think. Anyway, as we've discovered, Ed has a habit of making his side piece think he's going to leave his wife and marry her, and he didn't deviate from that pattern with Karen."

"Oh dear, please don't tell me that she um, did something desperate when she discovered Ed had lied."

I shook my head. "No, not that, but it was just as bad. Seems Karen decided to push Ed by getting pregnant, only it backfired and he broke up with her. Doctor Sawyer encouraged her, said it was a good thing, and that if she wanted the baby, he'd help her in any way he could."

"Sounds like Dad." Tate said. "Why don't I remember any of this?"

I shrugged. "Doris said Dean kept it all very quiet. As far as she knows, she's the only one other than Karen and Dean that knows."

Tate nodded. "Reasonable. If it was during the months after Mom died I can see how he was able to keep it a secret from me.

I was a mess and threw myself into my work. Took on lecturing at the college—anything to keep busy."

"Yeah, it was a rough time for both of you." Tate's mom had been killed by a drunk driver and the entire community had mourned her passing. She'd been an active and devoted volunteer at the youth center as well as an inspirational high school teacher.

Lost in thought, we all fell silent until Mama cleared her throat. "So, if this young woman didn't fall to despair, what happened to make you believe Dean is capable of killing Ed Whitten over her?"

I swallowed past the lump in my throat. "After Dean offered his support, Karen embraced her pregnancy. Doris said she was excited to have the baby, her depression eased and she was making plans for the future. When she was almost five months pregnant, Ed came back into her life."

"I don't understand. You said he dropped her because she was pregnant."

I nodded. "He did, but for whatever reason he decided he wanted her back. But there was a catch. He'd resume their affair but only if she got rid of the baby."

Tate's eyes widened. "But, you said she was five months—"

"Yeah. She was well into her second trimester and abortions over fourteen weeks required specific reasons for the procedure, which Karen didn't qualify for."

Tate nodded. "So what did she do?"

"Ed paid for her to go out of state but he didn't go with her, the pig. Doris didn't know all of the details about where she went or who performed the procedure, but regardless, something went wrong. Karen returned and developed an infection. Had she been treated right away, she would have survived, but she didn't seek treatment until it was too late. She died of septic shock."

"Oh no, how horrible!" Mama wiped at the tears staining her cheeks. "Why didn't she go to Dean for help?"

I shook my head. "We'll never know, but Doris seemed to think Karen didn't want to disappoint Doctor Sawyer. He'd been upset when she decided to go back to Ed but still supported her decision. Only, Karen didn't tell him about Ed's ultimatum."

"So she went off and had the abortion without telling anyone, then came home, developed an infection, and didn't seek help because she didn't want Dad to know what she'd done?"

I shrugged. "That's what Doris said. Either way, Karen died as a result of the abortion, and Dean found out that Ed had forced her to do it." I looked at Mama. "I can't believe you didn't hear about this. Doris said Dean went to Ed's house, dragged him outside, and beat the snot out of him."

Mama gasped. "I never heard a thing. But it's not surprising. Ed would have been humiliated. That's not something you want spread all over town."

"True. But the way news spreads in this town..."

"So Dad beat Ed up over this and that's why you think he killed Ed?" Tate scoffed. "It's a tragic story, but why would Dad kill him now? Why not then? And if he hated him so much and held him responsible for the woman's death, he'd never have bought a home off him!"

Tate made good points, but unfortunately I'd thought of them too and done some research. "He wouldn't have known Ed was backing the development, Tate. On a hunch, I did a little digging and seems Pine Harbor was marketed under a Crown Holdings. It was only after the marina and yacht club were opened that Ed let it be known he was the sole owner of Crown Holdings."

"Why would he have kept it a secret?" Mama asked.

"Can't say for sure, Mama, but probably had something to do with the environmental protests. I called Felicity and she said when they started the petitions, the only information they could find on the development company was an address in Delaware."

"This is unbelievable." Tate erupted, making me jump. "I can't believe you're actually sitting here telling me my dad is guilty of murder!"

"Tate, I'm not saying he did it, but you have to admit it's possible. There's the cufflink and then you add in his history of violence toward Ed...what he did to him that night at the gala. He was powerfully angry over the condo and when you add in their history...it's not a stretch to think he might have met up with Ed that morning, lost his temper and—"

"No!" Tate slammed his fist onto the counter. "No, this is all nonsense and I'm not going to stand here and listen to it any longer." He stalked to the door and stepped onto the porch. Just before he slammed the door, Tate growled. "Thanks for nothing, Holly."

Chapter Twenty-One

Dousing my face with cold water kick-started my brain but did nothing to alleviate my exhaustion. Tate's dramatic exit the night before had pierced my heart and left me crying myself to sleep. Not content with that level of misery, the universe had decided to resurrect my nightmare of the shooting.

What sleep I managed had come in fits and spurts, and now I was grumpy, miserable, and depressed. Lacking anything better to do, I decided to be productive and clean the house, after I tried one more time to get in touch with Tate.

I'd left several voice mails and sent numerous texts to Tate but he wasn't responding. Not that I blamed him. I didn't want to believe his father was guilty, either. But, unlike Tate, I could admit Dean had not one but two powerful motives.

The muscle memory required for mopping and dusting did little to shut down my brain, and I found myself thinking about Ed's murder and Dean's possible involvement on an endless loop.

The story of what happened to Ava's mother kept coming to the forefront of my mind. Several things bothered me—one being Ava herself. Where was she? I'd called my former boss soon after hearing Doris's tale and Craig had checked the files. There had been no reported sightings of Ava. No credit card usage and her cell phone was inactive.

She was missing, either by foul play or choice, but why? I also couldn't help but think about her relationship with Ed. He'd called her sweetheart, listed her as his wife on the fake passports, and had obviously planned to take her with him. Their relationship was serious, at least on Ed's part.

That led me to believe one of two things. Either Ava had no knowledge of Ed's relationship with her mother, or she did know and had been seeking revenge. The annoying voice in my head kept voting for revenge, but up until now I'd ignored it.

However, there was evidence to back up the idea. Ava and a huge sum of money went missing right after Ed's murder. Logic said she'd killed him and walked off with eight million, but the state of her condo didn't mesh with those facts.

Unless she staged the entire scene...once again my inner voice had a good point. If true, it was an elaborate and well-thought-out plan which led me to the case against Dean.

There was no denying Dean had attacked Ed at the ball and allegedly had done the same a decade or so ago. But both incidents had been spur of the moment. Doris said Doctor Sawyer had went to speak to Ed about Karen's death and it ended up in a fist fight.

The same scenario led to the fight on the dock during the Valentine's Day ball. Dean lost his temper and lashed out. But Ed's murder didn't read that way.

Aside from a trail of blood, there was nothing to indicate a struggle. Ed had been shot with the spear gun while walking toward his yacht which suggested he'd felt comfortable with whomever was there.

Just like that, I'd come full circle back to Ava. Frustrated, I pulled out the vacuum cleaner and attacked the dust bunnies. I was trying to shove the couch off the area rug when Dewey stomped into the living room raising kane.

"Hey," he shouted over the noise. "Youseenmyshin'pol?"

Frowning, I tried to decipher what he'd said with no luck. I turned off the machine. "What did you say?"

"I asked if you seen my fishin' pole."

I rolled my eyes. "Uh, in the garage like it's supposed to be?"

He scowled. "Nah, not that one. I bought me a new one with that gift card ya gave me for Christmas. Tracking says it was delivered yesterday, only I can't find it no wheres."

I shrugged. "Don't know, ask Mama." I started to turn on the sweeper but Dewey kept pestering me.

"Already did. She says she ain't seen it."

"Don't know what to tell you then."

His lower lip jutted out as he whined. "Come on, help me find it. Was supposed to meet Whopper at the marina twenty minutes ago."

Knowing my brother wasn't going to drop the subject, I gave in. "Look, use some logic. According to postal tracking, it's been delivered. Was it sent to this house?"

He huffed. "Well course it was, where else would it go?"

"If you're sure you put the right address down and it came here then look at what time it was delivered."

His brow furrowed. "Why's that matter?"

I rolled my eyes. "It matters because Mama and I were gone all day, which means the gates were closed. If they delivered before five, it was left at the gate."

Realization slowly dawned. "Shoot, ain't no package out there, I checked."

"Whelp, then it was probably stolen. Check the camera."

Dewey ran off to determine his fishing rod's fate and I returned to my self-appointed chores, but as I pushed the sweeper across the rug, what I'd sent to Dewey to do hit me between the eyes. Check the cameras.

Cameras watching over gates were common and if anyone would have them, it'd be a high-end resort complex like Pine Harbor and the Yacht Club. The police had requested footage from the marina, but were told they weren't operational yet. But what about the condo owners? It was possible someone's door camera had caught site of Ava.

With Mama tagging along to the marina office, I'd gotten distracted and neglected to ask about the gate code access records.

Curious to see who had accessed the docks that night and also wondering if any homeowners had cameras, I decided a trip to the island was infinitely better than a day of drudgery.

With luck, I'd find the missing piece to the jumbled mess that was wrecking my life.

Chapter Twenty-Two

Parking in the guest lot, I waved to Henry and pretended my destination was the yacht club, but once I saw him occupied with a delivery van, I changed direction and made my way to the condo complex.

The first wave of construction completed was six condos located near the marina. Two were waterfront with the others behind them laid out in a square around a central courtyard. John McGrath lived directly across from Ava's, so I started there.

After knocking several times with no response, I tried the others only to strike out again. I pivoted and made my way to the marina office, surveying the path as I went.

If someone living in the condos had killed Ed, they would have taken the path to the marina. It wound through lush landscaping, and any cameras wouldn't have a clear view until it opened up at the docks.

I let The Colonel sniff around as I examined the entrance to the docks. There was no gate at this entrance, but there was a camera mounted on a light pole. Shame they weren't operational.

I entered the office to find Bobby Raymond manning the desk. He was a straight shooter kind of guy and instinct said the direct approach would go over better than subterfuge.

"Mornin' Bobby. Life treatin' ya well?"

He smiled. "Can't complain. What brings you out here?"

"Hopin' you can help me." Counting on Dean's reputation in the community being persuasive, I explained that I was trying to help him beat a murder rap.

Bobby sighed and shook his head. "Bad business, this whole thing. Ain't no way Doc Sawyer killed anyone. Hope you figure out who really did it, Holly. Ed wasn't the greatest guy, but no one deserves that fate." He shuddered and stared out toward Ed's yacht. "Told him more than once karma would catch up with him, though."

Now that was interesting. "What did Ed do that made you say that?"

Bobby snorted. "You knew Whitten. Fancied himself a player and wheeler-dealer. Lots of people upset with his raping our landscape, and he also left a string of broken hearts in his wake. Between those things you could take your pick of people wanting him to get his comeuppance."

I had to agree. "Yeah, he didn't go out of his way to make friends but his murder...Bobby, whoever did it had to have access to this marina and from what I gather, that's only a handful of people."

He nodded. "Yep. That detective asked for a list but ain't heard nothing from him since they arrested Doc."

My brows shot up. "You made a list for Brannon and he didn't pick it up?" Bobby nodded and I saw red. Typical Joe Brannon. "You still have that list, Bobby?"

"Sure, you want it?"

"Please." He pulled a piece of paper from a drawer and slid it across the desk. "Thanks. These are all the members that have gate codes to access the marina?" There were only seven names. "Not many people for a club this size..." I continued to peruse the list as he explained.

"Not many docking their boats here yet. Only owners and yacht club officers have codes."

"I see," I muttered. The first three names on the list were as I'd expected. John McGrath, Ed Whitten, and Bobby Randall. After that, there were three names I didn't recognize and at the bottom of the list was Serena Osbourne.

"Bobby, who are these people and why are they on the list?" I pointed to the last four names.

He leaned over and pointed. "Brent Crawford owns that sport fisher bobbing in slip five; uh, Steve Adams has slip two; and Ms. Serena is the club treasurer." He glanced at me. "That help?"

Oh, indeed it did. Serena had straight up lied. Not only was she a member, but she was also a club officer. Why she lied was another story and I found out with my next question for Bobby.

"So how do you tell when a code has been used?"

He pointed to a string of numbers in a column. "This is the time stamp. Don't know why it's got all those other numbers but if you ignore the zeros you get the date and time, see?"

I did see, and only two people had used their code on February 14th. Ed Whitten was no surprise, but I did bat an eye at the other.

"Serena Osbourne used her code at 11:53 February 14th. Am I reading that right?"

Bobby frowned as he read the time stamp. "That's what the paper says. Wonder what she was doing down here that late. Only time she shows her face is if I don't send the fuel sale receipts on time."

"I take it you weren't late in sending those?"

He shook his head. "No ma'am. Turned 'em in the first Friday of the month like always. February sales ain't due until March."

"And you can't think of any other yacht club business that she'd need to enter the marina for?"

He again shook his head. "Nope, especially the night of the ball."

Chip, the kid that had helped me when Mama and I stopped in the first time, came out of another office. He didn't recognize me, thank goodness, and immediately started talking to Bobby about maintenance schedules.

I waited until he'd went to the computer behind the counter then asked Bobby about the camera by the path leading to the condos.

"Yeah, like I told the police, the cameras aren't online yet. They finished the install last month but they gotta come back to run some kind of test before they'll be operational. Shame, if those babies had been live we'd know exactly who killed Ed."

Since I already had a pretty good hunch who that was, I was just hoping for confirmation and proof, but a video wasn't going to provide it. I was turning to leave when Chip piped up.

"Hey Bobby?" We both turned to look at Chip. "Uh, I wasn't eavesdroppin' or nothin' but heard you tellin' the lady the security cams aren't online."

"Yeah, what about it?"

Chip flushed beet red and dropped his gaze. "Um, thing is, they are. I forgot to tell ya the tech crew came by first of the week and ran that diagnostic. Couple of 'em are workin' now but they gotta install a booster for the ones near the end of the docks. Wi-fi isn't strong enough."

My eyes widened. "Chip, which cameras are working? Can you pull the feed?"

214

Chip gulped and looked at Bobby, who nodded permission. Chip moved to the computer and started typing. "The gate cams and two along the main pier are hardwired. It's only the bluetooth ones that are still down."

He clicked on the screen and a video feed opened. Running across the screen were three windows, each showing a section of the marina. Beneath them were three more windows that I assumed were for when the non-functioning cameras came online.

The footage was grainy and black and white, but I could clearly make out the pier that led to the berths. The next window showed an angled view of the marina office that included the front door and part of the walkway that led to the fuel tanks. I looked at the next window.

Smiling like the cat who caught the canary, I pointed to the third window. "Chip, can you pull that camera's footage up from February 14th through the next day?"

He again sought permission from Bobby before complying. "Okay, here's the February 14th footage. Any particular time you're wantin' to see?"

I thought about his question. Ed was killed between 1:00 a.m. and 3:00 a.m., February 15th, but before I looked at the time of death, I was curious. "Show me Valentine's Day starting at 11:30 p.m."

Freezing rain had covered the docks that night and as expected, not a creature was stirring that late. I had Chip slowly advance the frames. "Stop! Can you zoom in?"

"Sure, it'll get blurry if I do too much though."

I watched the screen as he clicked the mouse. He zoomed in a few times and then we waited as the camera slowly captured the falling rain. Twelve minutes after midnight things got interesting.

"That's Ed!" Bobby exclaimed. "And ain't that Ms. Walker with him?"

Indeed it was. We watched as Ed gripped Ava's arm and helped her walk down the path that led to the condos. In his free hand, he carried a duffle bag that I'd bet my last nickel contained eight million in cold hard cash.

They passed the entrance camera and I marked the time as 12:22. A minute later they disappeared.

"Shame the dock cameras aren't online yet, we coulda seen who killed him."

I smiled at Chip. "If I'm right, we'll see them walk by this camera in a few, just wait."

And wait we did. We stared at the computer monitor for another twenty minutes before I detected movement at the edge of the camera's range. A few seconds later, Ed Whitten came into view.

Carrying the duffle bag, he walked toward the condos. We watched until he was out of frame and then I had Chip pause the video while I did some thinking.

I was ninety-nine percent positive the missing money had been in the bag Ed carried, but if he'd been planning to abscond to Aruba with Ava via his yacht, why not leave the means of starting a new life on board? He carried the money back toward the condos, so where was it now?

"Chip, hit play please." We again settled back to watch a flickering image of an empty dock, but this time we only waited a few minutes for something to happen.

"There's Ed; wonder where he went?" Bobby leaned closer to the screen, as if that would answer his question. "And doesn't look like he's carrying that bag this time."

I nodded as I kept my eyes glued to the screen. It was now 12:49 and Ed, empty handed, was heading in the direction of the yacht's mooring. He casually passed through the entrance and disappeared from view. But the frame was only empty for a minute before Ed came back.

He stood by the lamp post, looking around, then his head jerked up and he looked at something across from him. He shrugged, said something, and then threw his head back and laughed.

But the laughter quickly faded. He stood up straight and crossed his arms over his chest, glaring at something to his right.

"Who's he talking to?" Bobby asked.

"Whoever it is, he's not happy." Chip replied.

"I'm guessing his killer." I watched with bated breath as the one-sided conversation seemed to escalate. Several times he shook his head and started to walk toward the boats only to turn back and speak again. Two minutes after that, a gloved hand shot out and grabbed Ed's arm. He shook them off, made a shoving motion, and then strode in the direction of the boats.

A quick blur flew across the screen and then Ed clutched his chest and doubled over.

Bobby gasped. "Is that...was that..."

Mouth dry, I could only nod. Shoulders hunched and head down, Ed hobbled out of frame. The time stamp said 1:08. We let the tape roll for another five minutes but when nothing and no one else appeared, I had Chip advance it frame by frame.

My patience was rewarded. Eleven minutes after the camera caught Ed Whitten being fatally shot with a diving spear, Ava Walker passed the camera mounted by the entrance to the condo path.

"Hey, who are they?"

Staring at the screen, I said. "Bobby, you need to call Detective Brannon and tell him what we've found. Chip, make a copy of this just in case."

Both men followed my instructions, leaving me to ponder what I was seeing. Ava, accompanied by another woman, shuffled past the camera, heading toward the condos.

Wearing a long, dark coat, scarf, gloves, and what appeared to be a fur hat, her companion was bundled up like she was on a trek through the arctic. She also had her arm around Ava's waist almost like she was half carrying her.

I had Chip slow the feed and stared at the woman as they made their way out of camera range. Not only couldn't I tell the identity of the other woman, I also wasn't sure if she was helping Ava over the icy ground or forcing her.

Something about the woman's outfit was nagging at me. I had Chip freeze and zoom the frame showing Ava and the other woman. With the long coat, only the hem of a gown was visible. That told me the woman had likely attended the ball. Either that or she'd come outside in her nightgown.

The fur hat was unusual gear for the Lowcountry, even during a cold front, but there wasn't anything distinguishing about it. I moved on to the arm wrapped around Ava. A gloved hand had grabbed Ed just before he was killed. Circumstantial in a court of law, but I was positive the woman with Ava was Ed's killer.

I was also positive of her identity, though I couldn't prove it. Serena Osbourne's code opened the main marina gate at 11:53. No one else accessed the marina via that gate, and we'd watched the other entrance via the security camera. The only people that had passed through there during that time were Ed and Ava.

Where Serena had been for over thirty minutes I couldn't say, but common sense said she'd waited for Ed, talked to him, then shot him on the pier.

But common sense wasn't going to convict her. I needed proof.

"Chip, zoom in as much as you can...right there, please." I pointed to the gloved hand at Ava's waist.

The sleeve of her coat had ridden up and the cuff of the glove was slightly exposed along with her arm. And she was wearing something that sparkled in the light.

"Can you get any closer?"

Chip shook his head. "Sorry, that's it. What are you looking for?"

I pointed to the woman I believed to be Serena. "She's wearing a bracelet, and while I think I know who she is, a clearer shot of her jewelry would tell for sure."

Chip nodded and started tapping on the keyboard. "Okay, let me try something." A few minutes of typing and clicking on things with the mouse and he'd taken a screenshot of the frame.

I stared at the single image and frowned. "That's no better—"

"It will be." Chip opened another window on the computer. "If I lower the brightness, increase the contrast..." He moved the mouse across the screen at lightning speed and then sat back with a satisfied grin. "Better?"

Oh, it was indeed! He'd worked some kind of photo magic then cropped and increased the size...it was just as I thought. The bracelet had several charms dangling from it and confirmed my hunch. Serena Osbourne was on the dock the night Ed was murdered and she left in the company of the missing Ava Walker.

Bobby set the phone down and came back to the desk. "Did what you asked. Detective Brannon said he'd send someone by to pick up the DVD."

I blinked and stared at Bobby for a minute, absorbing what he'd said. "You told him what is on the video?"

"Yeah, said the patrol officer would be around and thanked me." Bobby shrugged. "Ain't that evidence or somethin'?"

I laughed, though I was far from amused. "Something like that, Bobby."

The Colonel was restless and I was stumped, so I told Bobby to wait on a uniform to pick up the DVD and took my dog for a walk, choosing the route I'd just watched Ava and Serena take.

The puzzle was complete except for two things: which one of them fired the spear gun and where was Ava?

Chapter Twenty-Three

That I couldn't definitively say whether Serena was Ava's kidnapper or accomplice stuck in my craw. I was also steaming over Brannon's lack of action. At the very least, the entire condo complex should have been swarming with officers searching for signs of Ava.

Regardless of her role in Ed's death, she was missing under worrisome circumstances, and to my knowledge, the detective for Noble County had found something better to do than hunt for her.

Which left me and my bulldog, who was feeling frisky. Twice I had to reprimand him for trying to pull my arm out of socket. I was surveying the courtyard and surrounding condos in a desultory fashion when he jerked me again and I gave in. "Come on, buddy, let's go home."

The word had a magical effect on my boy. He wiggled and pranced around until I pulled him onto the sidewalk that led to the parking lot. I was glad at least one of us was happy.

I'd found Ed's killer. Whether Serena or Ava, one of them had pulled the trigger, though I doubted the video evidence would be enough to convict, much less get Brannon off his butt and make an arrest.

I could confront her with what I'd found, but what would be the point? I had no power to arrest her and while I could prove she'd been on the docks that night...I needed Ava. Victim or co-conspirator, she was a witness, and with the proper incentives, she could help convict Serena. Conversely, Serena could do the same if Ava had done the deed.

What a mess. One suspect I couldn't touch, another MIA, and no clear idea why one or the other had killed Ed.

Sighing, I pulled out my phone and called Tate. I doubted he'd answer, but I could at least leave a voice mail. Regardless of the unresolved issues surrounding Ed's murder, the video should be enough to get Doctor Sawyer released and hopefully patch things up with Tate. That was good enough for me.

Tate's voice mail message played in my ear, making me grit my teeth. His ghosting me was becoming ridiculous. I'd followed the clues where they led. It was not my fault that one of them had suggested his father was guilty.

"...leave a message." Not the way I wanted to deliver good news but, whatever. "Tate, I'm at Pine Harbor and I found video evidence that Dean did not kill Ed. Tell your dad's attorney to request a copy of the camera feed from Bobby Randall because Brannon is ignoring what I found. Hope this helps..."

I ended the call and felt like shouting. I hated not knowing who killed Ed. I hated not knowing where Ava was. I hated that my relationship with Tate was in tatters...I snorted and told myself to get a grip. It stank to high heavens, but I'd have to be content with finding enough to clear Dean.

Deciding I'd earned a treat, I clucked my tongue to get The Colonel's attention and guided him across the pavement. We'd go to Scoops and Sweets and drown our sorrows in ice cream.

I'd just removed his leash and loaded him into the car when a scream rang out, followed by a gunshot. That had come from the condos. I'd spun around looking for the cause of the noise when I caught a glimpse of someone wearing a bright red coat running toward the sport's complex.

A red coat. I'd admired Serena's red coat...could I be so lucky? One way to find out! I snapped the leash back on The Colonel and started running toward the building as fast as my bum leg could manage. Halfway across the lot I remembered that I'd put my pistol in the glovebox when I dropped Mama at home.

My mouth went dry at the thought of carrying a weapon again. It had been hard enough to even put it in the car, but I'd been powerless when someone ran me off the road. If something should happen while Mama was in the car...

Another scream rang out followed by panicked shouts and pandemonium as a group of people raced past me. They'd been coming from the tennis courts. I grabbed my gun and took off.

"What's happening?" I yelled as several people ran past me.

A teen turned and ran backward as he pointed. "There's a crazy lady with a gun!"

"Get to the guard shack and call 911!"

The kid ran off and I considered my options. I was armed but I hadn't held, much less fired, my gun for over a year. The smart thing to do was wait for the police, but, as evidenced by the mess

I'd managed to make lately, no one could accuse me of being the brightest of bulbs.

On the lookout for the *crazy lady with the gun* that I was pretty sure was Serena Osbourne, I cautiously moved closer to the fence surrounding the tennis courts. Someone had been playing when the commotion started because the ball server was still lobbing in a rhythmic cycle and an abandoned racket had been flung near the net.

Looping The Colonel's leash around a palm tree and commanding him to stay, I crept farther into the island of shrubs and used them for cover as I scanned my surroundings and listened intently for any sign of movement.

The tennis courts stood between a building housing the gym and indoor pool and the outdoor pool and a small café. It was the middle of the week and Pine Harbor only had a few residents making it unlikely either area was occupied.

Whatever the reason Serena was running around the development with a gun, she'd pose little danger to the public. With that concern eliminated, I focused on possible hiding spots. Where was she?

Holding my gun in compressed ready position, I was searching for her red coat when another shot rang out and a woman screamed. It'd come from the other side of the court. I could just make out someone crouched down beside one of the café tables. I was thinking of a way to get to them when a gust of wind rustled the palms and Serena's long red coat.

In the blink of an eye, Serena was across the patio. I held my breath and waited for the shot, but to my surprise, she reached under the table and hauled out her prize. That solved the mystery of the missing Ava Walker, and unless there had been a falling out among thieves, it also told me who had killed Ed Whitten.

Serena was unaware she had an audience so I held the element of surprise, but she had a hostage. I crept closer to the tennis courts and prayed she didn't kill Ava before the police arrived.

The Colonel was whimpering but hadn't given away his position by barking, yet. I glanced over to see him straining at his leash. With the amount of weight he could put into tugging, he'd be free in minutes. I had to act.

I did the only thing I could think of. "Serena!"

She whipped around and scanned the complex. "Who's there? Stay back or I'll shoot!"

"Let her go!" I was guessing she'd had Ava since the night Ed died. She needed her for something, which meant my command was falling on deaf ears. It did serve the purpose of stalling for time though. "The police are on their way, put the gun down!"

Her answer was another shot in my general direction. It hit a palm tree a couple of yards to my right, scattering bark all over the place. By my count, she'd taken three shots, but this wasn't the movies. I had no idea what type of gun she had nor what capacity magazine.

Still, I had to keep her distracted. I started to yell another useless demand for her to drop the weapon when she started screaming at Ava.

"Where is it?" She wrenched Ava's arm to drive home her demand.

Ava cried out and struggled to get free but a slap from Serena flung her head back and knocked the fight out of her. I could hear her sobbing as Serena again demanded to know where something was. My bet was on the money Ed had stolen and a second later I was proven right.

"I don't know!" Ava cried.

I held my breath as Serena waved the gun at Ava and screamed curses. The Colonel barked. I hissed for him to be quiet but that only made him more frantic. He was pulling and tugging...the leash was going to snap and then I'd have two things to worry about.

Serena was escalating and the police showed no signs of arriving any time soon. I scanned the area, looking for a closer position. If push came to shove, I'd have to take a shot. My stomach rolled at the thought.

Fifteen yards from the women was another cluster of bushes. I could make it if Serena turned her back. I tensed, ready to bolt as soon as the coast was clear, but before I could make my move, Serena lowered her weapon and half dragged Ava onto the tennis court.

The move put her within range, but she was holding Ava so close to her that I couldn't risk taking a shot even if I wanted to. And I seriously didn't want to.

My hand started to tremble as my mind carried me back to that dark road. I could hear the ticking of the engine, see myself flipping the catch on my holster as I exited the car. I started to pant and my vision began to narrow...

Stop it! I drew a deep breath and shook my head. *Focus, Holly!*

I stared at the balls littering the court, concentrated on the rhythmic click of the empty ball server, and counted every breath I drew until I could draw a steady breath. Swallowing back bile, I forced myself to assess the situation.

Serena and Ava were arguing again. Serena was trying to pull her toward the exit and Ava was fighting her all the way. Serena was losing it. She needed Ava to find the money, but I didn't think Serena was going to hold it together much longer.

Calling myself every kind of fool, I rose and shouted Serena's name as I walked through the gate and onto the court. "Put the gun down and let's talk this out."

Serena turned toward me and then she laughed. "Should have known it was you. Can't keep your nose out of other people's business."

She was now only eight to ten yards from me. I held the gun behind my back and kept my body at an angle to her. I'd relinquished my cover, but I didn't have to give her an easy target. "That's me, nosey to a fault. I blame my mother."

Serena laughed, but it sounded more deranged than amused. "Good way to get yourself shot, but then you'd know all about that." She must have assumed I was no threat because she turned and slapped Ava as she continued to demand the location of the money.

Poor Ava had been put through the wringer. Her hair was sticking out at all angles and she was sporting a black eye. Her nose and lips were bleeding and she was in a T-shirt and leggings, both of which were torn and dirty. I couldn't let the assault continue.

"Serena! Put the gun down and let Ava go. She doesn't know where Ed hid the money, but I can make a guess."

She whipped around and leveled the gun on me. My heart stuttered in my chest and fight-or-flight reflexes were kicking in. This was not good, very not good! "Ah, lower your weapon, if-if you want to find the eight mil."

The patter of footsteps were closing in fast; The Colonel had freed himself and was coming to find me. My finger moved into firing position. "Serena, why did you kill Ed? For the money?"

At this point, I couldn't care less what had motivated her but training kicked in and said keep her talking. Where were the police?

Serena giggled. "You are really bad at this. I mean, all those glowing reports in the paper made you sound like a regular Sherlock but here you are, without a clue..."

From the corner of my eye, I caught sight of The Colonel. He'd be inside the court in seconds. I closed my eyes and said a silent prayer that Serena wouldn't shoot at him. If she even pointed in his direction, I'd drop her like a rock.

My chest was tight and I could hardly breathe, much less talk, but I willed the panic away and forced myself to think.

Years ago, when I was still a green-around-the-gills patrol officer, I'd answered a domestic call. A man was having a meltdown in his front yard and holding his wife at gunpoint.

I'd kept him talking until backup arrived by coaxing him into airing his grievances and making him think he was in control. I was hoping the same technique would work on Serena.

"So tell me then. How do I have it wrong?"

She glanced at me and snorted. "This the part where I confess?" She laughed and turned back to Ava, shaking her until her teeth rattled. "Where is the money?"

"Serena! I told you she doesn't know! Let her go and I'll take you to it!"

She scoffed. "Like you know, you've been wrong about everything else. Why should I believe you?"

I tensed as The Colonel came bounding up to me. As I reached out to grab his leash, he scampered away to the other side of the court. Great, he was ready to play. Hoping he'd occupy himself and stay out of harm's way, I turned my attention back to Serena. Thankfully, she seemed unconcerned with my dog's presence and I aimed to keep it that way.

"Believe me or not, it's up to you. Did you know there's a working camera at the marina? I watched Ed carry a large duffle bag somewhere. Put the gun down and I'll show you."

Oh, that got her attention. She released Ava and swung around, leveling the gun at me again. Keeping my eyes on her, I motioned with my free hand and hoped Ava took the hint and ran.

"Where is it? I know it's somewhere in this wretched development."

"Uh, your gun Serena. I'm not telling you squat until you put it down."

She stepped toward me and racked the gun. "I hardly think you're in a position to bargain. Tell me, or I'll shoot you..." Her gaze darted to someplace behind me and I winced. She'd spotted The Colonel. "Or, better yet, I'll shoot that dog."

Ava must have been in shock because she stood still as a statue, her hand pressed against her mouth as she fought back sobs. This was going sideways. I raised my gun and prepared to fire.

"Oh, look at you coming prepared to play. Think you're a regular Marshall Dillon." She smirked. "Nah, more like Barney Fife."

Ignoring her taunts, I narrowed my focus and cleared my mind. The soft whoosh of the ball server and Ava's cries helped ground me as I fought the rising panic. I was going to have to shoot her...

My finger was in position. I drew a deep breath, ready to release it as I squeezed the trigger. The Colonel barked and then a ball whizzed by me like a missile and hit Serena square in the head. She screamed and the gun fell from her hand.

"Get on the ground!" I raced over and kicked the gun across the court. "Serena, on the ground, arms out, do it now!"

"Ava, go sit down at the café." She stared at me, her eyes wide and vacant. "Move!" Hoping she'd comply, I moved closer to where Serena lay on the ground. I had no cuffs and I could finally hear sirens approaching so I lowered my weapon, kicked her legs farther apart, and sat down a few feet from her.

"My head...what hit me?" Serena mumbled.

I grinned and patted my leg until The Colonel lumbered over, another ball in his mouth. "That would be a tennis ball." She groaned, which made me laugh. "He just wanted to play."

Chapter Twenty-Four

Tossing the proof copy of tomorrow's paper aside, I smiled. "Thanks for keeping my name out of it, I owe you one."

Jessica grinned. "No problem, and I'll remember that." Her smile faded as her gaze ran over me. "You all right? You're looking a bit..."

"Rough?" I smirked. "You can say it, I've looked in the mirror."

Her brow furrowed. "What's wrong, coming down with something?"

I shook my head. "Nah, just not sleeping very well."

And that was a heck of an understatement. Once the cops showed up and arrested Serena, the adrenaline rush faded and I'd almost passed out. EMTs had wanted to transport me to the ER with Ava, but I'd waved them off and called Tate.

He'd come right away and took me home without scolding me, which I thought was progress. We'd been slowly mending our relationship but things were still a little awkward. I'd forgiven him, though there wasn't really anything to forgive, but Tate couldn't forgive himself.

"Still having that nightmare?"

I'd broken down and told Jess the PTSD had returned and managed to describe the newest parts of my flashback. She'd nagged me to make an appointment with Dr. Styles, but so far, I'd resisted.

"Yes, and before you say it, I'm not going to call my therapist. I finally got her to sign off on my settlement order, if I go in there and tell her what's happening she'll insist I start regular sessions again and tie it to my disability checks." I shuddered. "No, I can deal with this on my own."

Jessica huffed. "How? You're risking your health letting it go on like this. You have to have sleep!"

"If I could just figure out what's triggering the dream it'd stop! The PTSD got much better after Roland helped me remember what happened after I was shot."

Jessica frowned. "But you know what triggered it. You had to pull a gun on that nut job and she was holding one on you!"

I shook my head. "That was awful, but it's not the trigger." She looked skeptical so I explained my reasoning. "See, the part of the dream that really keeps me up at night is seeing those men carrying something from the bed of the truck and talking about burying it. Remember? I also see a lifeless arm in some of the dreams so I am pretty sure they were carrying a body. That part of the nightmare happened before the standoff with Serena."

Jess pursed her lips. "I don't know. What if what you're seeing isn't real? Like, just your subconscious bringing other stuff into what you know happened at the hunting camp?"

All things were possible, but something told me that wasn't the case. A dream like Jessica was describing was weird, like seeing yourself running through a maze in your underwear while a werewolf chased you. It was terrifying, but part of you knew it was a dream even while sleeping. This felt all too real.

Either way, I was tired of talking about it. Eventually, I'd figure out what the dream meant, but in the meantime, I didn't need any more hassles about seeing the therapist. I cleared my throat and changed the subject.

"So, Serena is claiming the heat of passion defense?"

Jessica took up the new topic with enthusiasm, as I knew she would. "Yes, can you believe it? Like a jury is going to buy that after she kidnapped Ava and held her hostage. That is anything but heat of the moment diminished capacity."

"Yep, besides, she confessed to me while we were waiting for the cops. I hate to take the stand, but I will if it means she gets first degree."

Jessica nodded. "Hopefully it won't come to that, but if it does, you'll be fine." She snorted. "Imagine killing a guy because he wouldn't marry you."

"Eh, it was a little more than that. She told me the first time I talked to her that the affair with Ed was nothing serious, but when I mentioned the rumor that they'd broken up because he wouldn't seal the deal, she laughed and said no woman in her right mind would expect that from Ed." I shrugged. "She was certain he was a confirmed bachelor and I think she was fine with that until she found out his plan to marry Ava."

"You think so? I just can't believe she wrecked her life over that. I mean, doing it because he double-crossed her I can see, but why care about the other?"

"Because she'd helped him embezzle the escrow account thinking they were going to start a new life in Aruba. That's why she killed him. If he'd just split the money with her and said good luck, I think he'd still be kicking. When she found out it was Ava getting that new life in paradise..."

Jess shook her head and sighed. "Imagine ruining your life over a guy, especially one like Ed Whitten! She should use the insanity defense. But, speaking of money...how did you figure out where he'd stashed the loot?"

I grinned. "Oh, that was all Mama. Remember when she was detained for snooping around on Ed's yacht? Well, when I questioned why she did such a foolish thing she proceeded to tell me all about the interior of Ed's boat before she got to the point. When the police still couldn't find the money, I got to thinking about what I'd seen on the video. I knew Ed had carried that duffle to the boat, then left with it, and then came back empty handed."

I snorted. "Still have no idea why he did that, but I was positive the money had been in the bag. Since it wasn't found at Ava's condo nor in the yacht club offices, stood to reason it was on the boat. And then I remembered what Mama had been rattling on about that day. She said seats in the lounge were tacky and the cushions crunched when she sat on them." I shrugged. "Pays to listen when she rambles I guess."

"Well, I'm just glad Doc Sawyer is off the hook. Shame about his condo though."

"Yeah, since the money's been recovered all of the down payments will be refunded, but there's doubt if the development will continue. That will make Felicity and her neighbors happy, I guess."

Jessica shook her head. "They better hold off the celebrations. According to the grapevine, J.T. Minton is thinking about taking over the project."

I scoffed. "Doubt Pine Harbor would get completed with him at the helm. He hasn't finished the Canary Wharf project yet and it's been almost two years!"

"True. Guess poor Doc won't get his waterfront condo, regardless."

I grinned. "Pretty sure he's all out of the notion now. Last I talked to him, he was putting most of the money into CDs and taking Mama to that new five-star resort they opened in the Bahamas."

"Oooh, that would be awesome. Although, I just read there's been a string of burglaries there. The police are stumped."

My brows rose. "Really? Think I'll talk Dean out of that trip then. Last thing any of us need is Mama playing detective again!"

We both laughed and then Jess updated me on her investigation into the county truck accident.

"Last time we talked, gosh I can't believe that's been weeks ago! Anyway, remember me telling you there was something hinky with the service records for that truck?"

"Yes, you said the VIN number matched a new truck. Did you get the records you requested?"

She grinned. "Did I! I've been pouring over all of them but it's the purchasing forms I'm really interested in. Holly, there are twelve vehicles with questionable pedigrees, and every one of them was purchased from that rundown dealership out on Highway 70."

I frowned. "The one across from the dairy isle, right? It's kinda shady looking and the cars for sale never seem to change?" Jess nodded. "Who owns that?"

She smirked. "Don't know, but I aim to find out. But that's not all. All of the fraudulent trucks were requisitioned by Preston Spruill."

I sucked in a breath. "Are you thinking what I am?"

"If you're thinking Spruill bought all of those toys with the ill-gotten gains he got for defrauding the county by claiming to buy new trucks but changing the VIN numbers on old ones, then yes I am."

My brows rose as I considered what she'd discovered. "That kind of scheme has a lot of moving parts. He wasn't doing it alone."

"Exactly. That's why I'm digging into that car lot. Whoever owns it has to be involved."

"Isn't it listed on the business license?"

Jess laughed. "Girl, it's an umbrella corp. and so far I've tracked it to a PO Box out of Delaware, but the officers listed don't exist. I find it hard to believe the secretary of state's office didn't catch it, but that's government for you." She rose and gave me a hug. "I've got to run. You get some sleep and call me if you need to talk."

I assured her that I would and waved as she pulled out of the driveway. The crazy cold front had passed as quickly as it had come and now we were experiencing a false spring. I was contemplating a run to It's About Thyme for some bedding plants when Dewey stomped onto the porch and flopped down beside me on the swing.

Stretching his legs out and crossing them at the ankles, he put his arms behind his head and sighed. "Man, it's a beautiful day."

I cocked a brow and pointed at the trail of muddy footprints he'd left. "Better enjoy it while you can. When Mama sees the mess you made on her freshly painted porch she'll take a broom to your backside."

He glanced at the mess and grimaced but then he shrugged. "Nah, I'll just tell her you did it."

My mouth fell open. Dewey grinned and waggled his brows. I laughed and nudged him in the ribs. "Brat!" We both laughed in a way I couldn't remember us doing in a long time.

It was nice. My brother and I had a good relationship on the whole, but it was often adversarial. We squabbled like the kids we used to be. That had changed over the last few weeks and I thought I knew why.

I swiped at my eyes and chuckled again. "What's put you in such a good mood?"

His smile was smug. "Got a date."

My smile went from ear to ear. "I see, wouldn't be a certain little history buff by chance?"

Dewey gave me a side-eye. "How'd you know?"

"Please," I rolled my eyes. "She's all you talk about. Penelope this, Penelope that, Penelope says..."

He frowned. "I don't do that!"

"You so do."

"Do not."

"Do so..."

We bantered back and forth with Dewey ending it by shrugging his shoulders and sticking his tongue out at me. "Okay, I do. So what?"

I chuckled. "Nothing wrong with that. I think she sounds great. Can't wait to meet her."

Dewey grinned. "She is, and man is she smart! Did I tell you what Penelope said?"

He didn't give me a chance to answer, launching into the history of Myrtlewood as interpreted by the museum curator. "...and the outbuildings were probably slave cabins at some point. Penelope says there's so much history preserved at Myrtlewood that we could make it a museum!"

I hid my smile so as not to deflate Dewey's enthusiasm, but Penelope's idea wasn't new. My father had considered opening Myrtlewood as a living history and educational center. In fact, he'd drafted a business plan and had been talking to schools and such to determine interest. A premature heart attack had ended that dream but it was always in the back of my mind.

I wondered how Dewey didn't know that, but upon reflection I admitted that Dewey was a mama's boy and he tended to be self-centered. I doubt he had ever sat and listened to Daddy's plans.

If it took a pretty face to pull him from his self-absorption so be it. Having exhausted his dissertation on Penelope's opinions and virtues, Dewey quieted. We sat in comfortable silence, enjoying the beautiful weather until my gaze fell on the muddy footprints.

Curious, I asked. "So, how *did* you get so dirty?"

Dewey chuckled. "Took Penelope out to Myrtlewood. The yard is a mess from all the digging and stuff, but the university was able to get use of the ground penetrating radar gizmo again so they were out looking for more gravesites and she wanted to watch."

He twisted in his seat. "Did I tell ya they've found fifteen sets of remains so far? Penelope says it was likely an old grave-yard that somehow got destroyed. Aint' no records of it being there but she says that's the only reasonable explanation." He shrugged. "I got no idea, but she's excited. Says it's a historical find worthy of a paper, whatever that means."

"It means she wants to write an academic paper about the dig and its findings." I yawned and wished I could go back to bed. Not that there was any point. I'd just have another nightmare.

Dewey shrugged and I let the matter drop. My brain was working out the problem that was preventing me from sleeping. Why was this happening? Why now? Something must have triggered...I blinked and looked at Dewey.

"What did you say? I was daydreaming."

He snorted. "I was just tellin' ya about the bones they found in one of the graves. Penelope is all excited because this one was buried with some stuff she says is common in Gullah culture. And whoever it was must have been important because there's fragments of a shroud? I didn't know what that was but Pene-lope said it's like a cloth or tarp...hey, what's wrong? You're lookin' kinda pukey." He scooted across the seat. "Ain't comin' down with somethin' are ya? I don't wanna get sick!"

I scowled and shook my head. "No, it's not that, I'm thinking..." Dewey's description of the recent discovery was interesting but when he mentioned the shroud, or tarp as he called it, a light bulb went off.

"Dewey? Is the university still out at Myrtlewood? Are they still using that ground penetrating whatsit?"

He frowned. "Yeah, at least they were still there when we left. Penelope had a meeting so we took off but pretty sure Professor Stanley said they only have the use of the machine for a couple a days, so they plan to work until dark—hey, were ya goin'?"

"To borrow that machine."

Chapter Twenty-Five

The gang, minus Connie, was all here. I'd called them all while I drove to Myrtlewood, asking them to meet me at Roland's hunting camp with only the briefest of explanations. As we watched Professor Stanley and his team operate what looked pretty much like a lawn mower with a computer tablet attached to the handle, I elaborated.

"I've already told Jess this, but the reason I asked y'all to come out here is because my PTSD has returned with a vengeance." I proceeded to tell them an abbreviated version of the nightmare plaguing me.

Tate sucked in a breath. "Why didn't you say anything? You need to resume your sessions with—"

"And that is exactly why I didn't say anything." I smiled to take the sting out of my words. "Tate, the focus therapy Dr. Styles taught me helped tremendously, but the rest?" I shook my head. "It had no effect on the flashbacks."

I nodded at Roland. "The reason my issues lessened was because of your help in remembering what happened out here. I fully believe that and it's why I asked Professor Stanley to run his radar thingy. A repeating theme in that awful dream is two men lugging a tarp from the back of what we now know was Preston Spruill's truck and talking about a shovel."

I pointed across the dirt road where the university team were walking in a grid pattern, watching the radar screen. "We are standing where I was shot. Y'all saw me lie down in the general area I fell when I was shot and lifted my head, just as I would have done that night. My theory is they buried someone over in that general direction and I want to know who it was."

Tate mumbled something about my stunt nearly killing me but I ignored him. Reenacting my position after being shot had definitely affected me, though I did my best to hide it. My heart still hadn't returned to a resting rate and any moment I thought I might vomit.

However, I'd do whatever it took to find the truth and my gut said this was the only way.

We watched in silence for another twenty minutes before a shout alerted us the team had found something. As we approached the team, Roland cautioned. "This is old Indian ground and my family has been hunting here for decades. They could have found animal remains, or old ones like you discovered at Myrtlewood. Let's not get our hopes up."

I nodded but chose not to argue. My inner radar was clanging to beat the band. I was positive they'd found fresher remains. A minute later, my instincts proved sound.

"You were right, Holly." Professor Stanley pointed to the radar screen. "We have a body, not bones. Whoever the poor soul is, he hasn't been down there more than a year, year and a half at most."

I nodded and looked at Tate. "You're the coroner. Can we start digging or do we have to wait for your tech team?"

Tate met and held my gaze. I needed no words to understand what he was thinking. I quirked a brow and offered an apologetic smile. "I'm gonna be in a bad way, regardless, Tate. At least knowing who it was lets me move forward..."

He stared at me a moment longer and then scowled. "On your own head then. Shovels are in the back of Roland's truck. Shake a leg, ya'll."

Under Tate's direction, we carefully excavated, guided by the radar image. They hadn't buried the unknown soul very deep. Thirty minutes of digging and we had enough exposed for Tate to do a preliminary examination.

I struggled not to gag as he brushed aside the last of the soil. Decomp had started with a vengeance, but Tate merely hummed and continued sifting, sorting, and probing at what remained. After an agonizingly long time to my anxious mind, Tate removed something from the pocket of the body's jeans and got to his feet. "The victim is male, estimate he's in his midthirties, and died from a gunshot wound to the back of the head." He handed me a pair of gloves. "Put these on and take a look at this."

I did as instructed and he laid a brown leather wallet in my hand. It was tattered around the edges but in remarkably good condition. I hoped whatever was inside had been similarly preserved.

"Go on, open it. Let's see if this guy had ID on him."

I frowned at Dewey for rushing me, but conceded it was time to bite the bullet. Drawing a deep breath and bracing myself for whatever I was about to discover, I opened the wallet and gasped.

Nestled behind a plastic window was a perfectly legible driver's license.

"Well, who is it?"

I met Jessica's gaze and swallowed hard. "Preston Spruill."

I hope you enjoyed spending the Valentine's season with Holly, The Colonel, and all of her friends. If so, why not leave a review to help other's discover Sanctuary Bay?

Chapter Twenty-Six

Hey neighbor, new to the area? Holly and her friends have had several adventures!

Back when Holly was still a Noble Count Sheriff's Deputy, she tracked a ring of thieves and met The Colonel. Find out how Holly's little buddy got his name by reading the prequel novella, **Hounds and Heists**!

Visit www.rachellynneauthor.com to read this snippet of Holly's past for **FREE** as an eBook or find it in paperback on Amazon.

Holly has moved on from her law enforcement days and started *CoaStyle,* but decorating for events has certainly not led to a slow and safe lifestyle!

Following her debut as a decorator in **Masquerades and Murder**, Holly went on to create a Christmas market for the town in **Carolers and Corpses** and then tracked a killer to

Sandpoint Abbey after a priest died during the Blessing of the Fleet.

You'd think our reluctant sleuth could catch a break by decorating for a wedding in **Plantations and Allegations** but, as The Colonel says, the *Lady that Pays the Bills* finds trouble wherever she goes.

Lucky for Holly her bulldog is always on the case!

After surviving the events surrounding the *wedding of the year*, Holly took a much needed vacation and then celebrated the cooler weather by organizing a fall festival.

But, with a corn maze full of **Scarecrows and Scandals** she's sure to find herself in the thick of things!

There will be 12 books in the Holly Daye Mystery Series as our decorator friend fills her calendar with clients and slowly unravels the secret behind the shooting that ended her law enforcement career.

Stay tuned, it promises to be a wild ride!

Chapter Twenty-Seven

<u>The Holly Daye Mystery Series</u>

<u>Hounds and Heists</u>

<u>Masquerades and Murder</u>

<u>Carolers and Corpses</u>

<u>Priests and Poison</u>

<u>Plantations and Allegations</u>

<u>Scarecrows and Scandals</u>

<u>The Cosmic Café Mystery Series</u>

<u>Fey Goes to Jail</u>

<u>Ring of Lies</u>

<u>Holly Jolly Jabbed</u>

<u>Broken Chords</u>

Chapter Twenty-Eight

Hey y'all!

Since you've finished my book, it'd be redundant to tell you that I'm a writer. But I'm also a mom, a grandma, a housewife, and a former grocery worker; all titles I proudly hold!

I wrote my first book, Ring of Lies in 2011, got the idea for Broken Chords and wrote a few chapters and then promptly let life get in the way. I did volunteer work while I home-schooled my daughter and helped my husband start a business but, when she decided to attend high school, I decided to find work outside the home.

I was managing a department in a grocery store, (which I loved doing) and I'd find myself writing stories while I put away stock; there is something about muscle memory work that lets the subconscious play. I started carrying a sharpie in my pocket along with my box cutter and, when I'd get an idea, a snippet of conversation between characters, or a creative way to axe someone I'd scribble it on a piece of cardboard!

As much as I loved my job, I realized I had some pretty good ideas on those scraps of empty boxes and that is when I quit and started writing full time. To date, I have 8 books published with many more to come: there's no stopping me now!

All of my books take place in and around the Lowcountry of South Carolina and Georgia because that is where I call home and I am in awe of this region's natural beauty and its history.

Join my newsletter, The Cozy Crew Club, by going to www.rachellynneauthor.com. You'll hear more than you probably ever wanted to know about the Lowcountry and its unique culture.

On my website you'll also find links to my Facebook and Instagram pages. Follow me and you'll see my crazy menagerie of animals, the day trips my husband I take, recipes, chapter readings, and more!

Hope to meet you soon!

Rachel

Made in the USA
Columbia, SC
02 November 2024

45544769R00146